D0463531

WHAT WOULD
JESUS PRAY?

A STORY TO CHANGE THE WORLD

MACK THOMAS

Multnomah® Publishers *Sisters, Oregon*

WHAT WOULD JESUS PRAY?

published by Multnomah Publishers, Inc.

© 2006 by Multnomah Publishers, Inc.

International Standard Book Number: 1-59052-738-0

Interior illustrations by Bettina Burts

Multnomah is a trademark of Multnomah Publishers, Inc., and is registered in the U.S. Patent and Trademark Office.

The colophon is a trademark of Multnomah Publishers, Inc.

Printed in the United States of America

For information:

MULTNOMAH PUBLISHERS, INC.
601 N. LARCH ST.
SISTERS, OREGON 97759

06 07 08 09 10—10 9 8 7 6 5 4 3 2 1

Contents

A Word of Explanation 4

Part One: Before Midnight 7

Part Two: Before the Dawn 77

Seven Steps, Seven Stars 157

What Would Jesus Pray?—
Where to Find It in the Bible 160

In this story, there's a guy named Stefan who quotes a number of verses from the Bible. Stefan knew these words by heart. But he lived in the days before the Bible was divided into chapters and verses. Therefore no reference numbers are given in the story. But if you want to know where these passages are, there's an index in the back of the book, under the heading "Where to Find It in the Bible."

Part One

BEFORE MIDNIGHT

9:06 P.M.

A jolt of pain shot through Tyson Vasser's left ribcage as he tossed his backpack onto the rear seat of the junkpile that was Adam Kohek's car. Another jolt—even worse—stabbed again through his side as he dropped his tired body onto the seat.

He held his breath from the ache as he found a place for his feet amid the football gear and empty energy drink cans and motor oil bottles that cluttered the car's back floorboard. Tyson's pain was due to a soccer injury in this afternoon's junior varsity game—from a kick that hammered him after he tripped and fell right in front of an opposing player.

Tyson closed his eyes and gave his hurt some glory by imagining that it was a warrior's wound. *From the blow of a knight's lance*, he thought to himself, as he slowly leaned back his head. The enemy rider had caught his blind side while Tyson was engaged with soldiers in front of him. The hit could have been deadly, but somehow it failed to knock him

7

from his horse. He clutched his shield tighter to his wounded side, raised his sword in his right hand, roared out a battle cry, and hurled himself into the

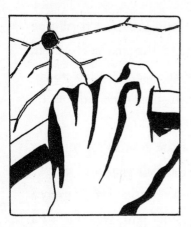

fight with more fury than ever. Like a man possessed.

"Shut the *door!*"

It was Adam Kohek, yelling at him from the driver's seat.

Tyson broke off his dreaming, reached for the handle, and slammed the door, all of which did nothing for his injured ribs.

Adam, shaking his head in irritation, sped out of the parking lot. He was stiff-arming the steering wheel. Tyson noticed that the guy's huge knuckles were tight, like he was throwing a punch frozen in time. Nobody in the car could miss Adam's mood, and they all stayed quiet.

Adam Kohek's sister, Natalie, was with him up front, sitting just ahead of Tyson. And Jared Paydell was with Tyson in the back. They were all freshmen at South High, except for Adam, who was a senior and played noseguard on the football team.

In this dented-up, chocolate-brown Toyota Corolla from out of the '80s, Tyson was thinking how weird it was to be riding with these three particular people tonight. Definitely unusual being with Adam—since SHS football players tended to snub the soccer guys, and seniors ignored freshmen even more.

But for Tyson, being here with Jared and Natalie was just as surprising. They weren't close friends. They happened to be taking freshman choir together, and the choir had been singing tonight at the annual Appreciation Dessert for parents of ninth graders. That's why Tyson stayed at school after the soccer game, even though his mom and dad didn't come to the dessert. Neither did Jared's or Natalie's parents, for that matter.

When the program was finally over, Tyson and Jared were out in the school lobby and both boys asked Cody Reznik if they could borrow his cell phone and call home for a ride. Natalie and Adam were passing by right then and overheard them—Adam had come to pick up his sister. Natalie asked her brother to drive the boys home as well, but when Adam agreed, he did it with what Tyson thought was a fake smile. Or maybe a smirk. Like this was only some assignment for him to earn good behavior points in somebody's book.

Anyway, whatever hospitality Adam possessed was definitely depleted by the time they all got in the car. Maybe it was how Tyson smelled. He hadn't bothered to shower after the game, and it was sweltering where the choir was singing—on risers, and under spotlights. Tyson sniffed one of his armpits. Yeah, that could be it.

But something else was even weirder about tonight, in Tyson's view. At unusual times recently—like late at night, or in the shower in the morning—two people kept popping into Tyson's mind. Those two were Natalie Kohek and Jared Paydell. Tyson figured there were good reasons for this. Natalie first caught his attention in a health class discussion when she said her parents were going through a divorce. She said it calmly, but everybody could see through her mask.

Earlier, Tyson had concluded he would never like Natalie because she was so serious; maybe she was overwhelmed by the changes from junior high—

which seemed stupid to Tyson, since he himself liked high school about a thousand times better. But after health class that day, he saw Natalie with different eyes. So he gave himself a mission to cheer her up whenever he got the opportunity.

Several times this fall, seeing her at lunch or in the hallway or after school, he'd spoken just the right little greeting or joke or crazy comment to melt her frown and bring a sparkle to her eyes, if only for a moment. She sent him a couple of e-mails to say thank you. Besides that, they never really talked. Tyson thought he'd done a lot for her, but tonight she seemed gloomier than ever.

Jared, meanwhile, had caught Tyson's attention the same way he got everybody else's—just by being the young brother of Scott Paydell, a senior on the school's state champion football team two seasons ago. Scott was remembered as the best running back ever to play for South High, and he even got a full-ride football scholarship to Penn State. But several weeks ago, late one Saturday night as he was driving home after a Penn State game, he was killed. It was foggy, and the car he was driving slammed into the back of a slow-moving semi truck climbing a hill on the interstate highway.

Tyson remembered hearing the details from his dad, who read them aloud from the newspaper. The car hit so hard that it was crushed and stuck beneath the heavily loaded truck, and got dragged along until the truck driver could stop. It gave Tyson nightmares about being in a car on a foggy night where the same thing happened. It was so horrible, and the whole town felt the tragedy.

Tyson remembered thinking how impossible it seemed that a guy as cool and strong and alive as Scott Paydell could be gone from this earth just like that.

Scott was the only brother Jared had, and after losing him, Jared missed a lot of school for a while. Tyson heard that Jared's mom had a history of mental problems, and that now they were worse.

On the day Tyson saw Jared back at school, he gave himself a mission for Jared as well. He decided to be a support. It didn't happen often, and Tyson felt he was mostly in the dark about what he could do or say to make any difference. But he tried. When Jared quit the football team—because the whole scene reminded him too much of his brother—he joined the cross-country squad, and Tyson went to a couple of his meets to cheer him at the finish line.

Now and then, in those quiet moments when Jared or Natalie came to his mind, Tyson would say a quick prayer for them. Nothing long or deep, just a special request for God to look after them and help them somehow.

On the windshield of Adam Kohek's car, there was a shatter-spot in the upper left corner, a small hole with cracks radiating down. Tyson's eyes were drawn to it. Every time they passed beneath a streetlight, it made faint rainbow colors along the cracks. He wondered if Natalie had noticed it. But she was only staring out the passenger window—maybe at the moon, three-quarters full, rising above the eastern hills.

He glanced at Jared, who also seemed deep in thought. Maybe it was their research reports due in history tomorrow. Tyson hadn't even started his yet. *Good thing I do my best work under pressure*, he thought. Still, it might be a long night. Maybe he and Jared could work on it together.

Tyson leaned over and asked him, "You started that paper yet for Mr. Miller?"

"*Shut up,*" Adam snapped from up front. His words weren't that loud, but they were plenty intense. Natalie gave her brother a stormy look for a moment, then turned back to stare out her window.

Jared looked at Tyson, gave a nod toward the back of Adam's neck, then shook his head with an expression that said, "Forget that jerk."

Tyson, however, was ticked. He honestly didn't feel like talking much tonight. He was tired and sore after a long day. But now that Adam was making an issue of it, Tyson was determined to speak up.

He kept his voice controlled. "So tell me, Adam. Why did you offer us a ride if you hate having us here so much?"

Adam braked hard. Before the tires quit screeching, he'd thrown back his arm and clutched Tyson's T-shirt at the neck. Tyson smelled his breath, and felt the heat of it, and saw the fire in Adam's eyes— but something else was there too. Something more like fear. *This is unbelievable.*

They stayed like that for a long, silent moment. Tyson finally took a breath. He grew conscious of Natalie's presence as she stared at her brother with her hands stretched open near her face.

A car went around from behind them, and the driver laid on his horn as he passed by.

The look in Adam's eyes went somewhere else, somewhere far off. He let go of Tyson, turned back around, and stiff-armed the steering wheel again with his left hand while he shifted gears with his right. They drove off.

After a few minutes, they reached Tyson's house. A light was on above the side door, and Adam pulled into the alley that ran next to it. Nobody said anything. Tyson gave a quick nod to Jared as he grabbed his pack, opened the door, and hurried out.

Adam's car peeled out before Tyson got the door closed, but he got a glimpse of a lost expression on Natalie's face as she looked up at him through her window. The car raced down the alley, turned into the street, and disappeared.

What a weird deal, Tyson thought. He was glad that was over.

Tyson flipped the light switch as he stepped from the alley into his house. Just inside the door was a small sink with a mirror hanging above it, and a single-bulb light fixture above that. The tiny room also held a washer and a dryer stacked over with laundry baskets full of Tyson's clothes, plus a stand-up freezer with his snowboard leaning against it.

Keeping a finger on the light switch, Tyson studied his reflection in the mirror, trying to see his face through Natalie's eyes. He shifted his jaw and tightened his brow to recapture his expression from a moment ago when she looked at him through the car window. He wondered, as he turned his head slowly from side to side, how good-looking she thought he was.

Then he leaned closer to the mirror, widened his eyes, and dropped open his mouth to reproduce the way Natalie must have seen him while Adam was clutching his shirt. He hoped it wasn't panic or weakness that she observed in him in that moment. He couldn't have hidden his shock, but maybe she detected nothing worse.

He turned off the light and opened a door into the kitchen. His dad was sitting there in a sweatshirt and jeans. Before him on the table was an empty cereal bowl and a spread-out newspaper.

"Waiting for your call," his dad said matter-of-factly.

"Got a ride," Tyson answered, as he dropped his backpack to the floor and sank into a chair across from his father. He tried not to grimace from his pain as he reached behind him to grab an orange from a basket on the counter.

"Mom in bed?" Tyson asked.

"Yeah. She's gonna try getting into work tomorrow morning. She felt a lot better today." Both of Tyson's parents had super-early jobs—his mom was a baker in a donut shop and his dad had the first shift sorting mail at the post office. But lately his mother had missed so much work due to a lower back injury that she was afraid of losing her position.

Tyson pulled out a chunk of the orange peel with his teeth.

"You look beat up," his dad said. "Are you hurt?"

Tyson took a deep breath that pained his side. "Nah. But the game was tough. We lost 3-2, and I missed four shots. At least." Tyson worked the peel with his thumb, taking it all off in one long, unbroken spiral.

"Well, at least you're taking the shots. Your mom and I can't wait to see you in Saturday's game. It's against Catholic, right?"

"I think so. And they're good." Tyson popped two orange sections in his mouth and savored the bursting juice as he bit into them.

"You know," his dad continued with half a smile, "I think you smell even worse than you look."

"Oh. Got busy after the game. No shower." Tyson gave his dad one of the orange sections.

"Thanks. And that dessert thing tonight? How was that?"

"Ah, you and Mom didn't miss much. It dragged on forever. Mom's back would have been killing her."

His dad swallowed the orange slice and took off his glasses. "So who drove you home?"

"Adam Kohek." Tyson saw that the name didn't register with his dad. "He's a senior. Plays football. Defense. Lives a few blocks over, across Belmont."

His dad rubbed his eyelids with a thumb and forefinger.

Tyson tried to head off a lecture. "I'm sorry, Dad. I should have phoned you first. Adam was there to pick up his sister, and he offered me and Jared Paydell a ride. We came straight home. Adam's okay."

His father sighed. "Ty, you know we don't mind you getting a ride, but first we need to know who with."

"I know. I'm sorry."

His dad dropped his right palm on the newspaper. "There's kids out there that… I was just reading about this house on Camden that burned Sunday night. They think it was arson. Some kids broke in and stole some guns and a lot of stuff, and shot these people's dog right there in the house. And then tried to hide their crime by torching the place." His dad shook his head in disgust.

Ty couldn't imagine any of his friends being that cruel or brainless. "How do they know kids did it? And how do they know it was more than one?"

"You wait and see. Besides, who else is that immature? And doesn't it come out most when they're together? They egg each other on from dumb to dumber, and suddenly a stupid stunt turns into a serious crime."

"Dad, I don't get mixed up with lowlife losers like that."

"I know, Ty. I know you don't *intend* to. You're more level-headed than most kids your age, but you still gotta be careful."

Tyson crossed his arms. He could see his dad's point.

"So next time?" his father asked calmly.

"Next time, I'll call. Promise."

"Thank you, Ty." His dad stood up from the table. "Well, time for me to crash." He folded the newspaper and added it to a stash of several others in the narrow space between the refrigerator and some cabinets. Then he took his bowl and spoon to rinse them under the faucet. "Got much homework tonight?"

"Yeah. A big report in history. Might take a while. But I finished everything else this afternoon after the game."

"Tell me, Ty. In all your busyness right now—are you taking time to get alone with God?"

Tyson slowly tipped his chair on its back legs. "Not enough. Not really."

His dad didn't press the issue, and Tyson was glad for that.

"What's your history report about?"

Tyson knew his father was a history buff. "Maybe you can help me on this." He reached in his pants pocket and pulled out a folded paper. He opened it and read the assignment: "Minimum of 500 words—describe some tool or technology that is essentially the same today as it was a thousand years ago, and explain why you think it hasn't changed much over that time."

His dad faked a groan. "Oh, I'm hurt! You actually think I'm that old?"

Tyson laughed. "No, really—got any suggestions?"

After a few seconds of silence, his dad exclaimed, "I got it!" He raised his hand, still holding a spoon, above his head.

"What?"

"This!"

"*What?*" Then Tyson understood. "Yeah, right! No way I could write five hundred words about a spoon."

"Well then, throw in a knife and a fork. Plus the bowl. A cup and a plate maybe." His father stood in the doorway to the hall and twirled his arms in a little invisible juggling act.

Tyson grinned. "Yeah, yeah, I get the picture. Oh well, I may go with that if I don't hit something better real fast. But Dad, come tell me if you're struck by a good idea—for real—before you nod off."

"Sure thing. Good night, son."

A few minutes later, Tyson was sitting in front of his computer at the desk in his bedroom. Above the desk was a shelf crowded with stacks of CDs, a half-burnt candle, and Tyson's collection of (mostly cheap) sunglasses. He set the unfolded paper with his history assignment next to the candle. Then he propped up his legs on the bed beside his desk.

He tapped the keyboard with his left hand as he gingerly rubbed his sore ribcage with his right. The last thing he felt like doing was writing a history paper, so he decided to chat a little first.

He got connected, and quickly received three messages.

One was from Jared:

→ dude thats cool the way you spoke up to adam kohek. is he cracked or what? hey talk to me if you have the time. got home and my mom has lost it again over my brother's death and this time i couldnt take it anymore. i dont know what to tell her right now because i have to deal with this too, anyway i need to talk if you can spare the time. thanks man. :Q

Another was from Natalie:

→ Sorry Tyson about my brother tonight. I'm very very scared for him and also for me. Something has happened, Adam is in serious trouble. I just found out today and he won't let me talk about it but I have to tell someone. I am so afraid.....

The third one popped up from some total stranger to Tyson, someone labeled "Stefan"—

→ I fear the worst. I see only danger and death before this night is ended. Help me! Come and help me!

Holy smoke, Tyson was thinking. He hardly knew where to begin. Yes, this could be a long night.

9:49 P.M.

Should he maybe flip a coin? Heads he'd answer Natalie first, tails for Jared. And if the quarter landed on its edge, he could start with that Stefan guy.

Or go alphabetical. Jared, Natalie, Stefan. Yeah, that was it.

He reread Jared's words. He wanted to help, but he had no idea how to answer him. He just didn't know. But he had to write something.

→ Yeah that was crazy with Adam. Hey Jared I was going to check with you on that history report. You probably finished it days ago. Got any leftover ideas I could steal from you???? Wish I knew what to say about your mom and all. I guess the pain of losing someone never heals fast. But hey I don't want to sound like I know all about it. I don't. Can't think of anything worse— a mom losing a son, a guy losing his only brother. I don't know how you deal with it.

That probably doesn't help you much but
Jared I can listen….

Then a quick word to Natalie. It bothered him how
scared she seemed.

→ No need to apologize for your brother.
I guess I figured something big must be eating
at him. I don't really need to know what it is
if you can't tell me. But please please don't be
afraid Natalie. Just be calm.

That didn't seem strong enough or helpful enough.
He added more:

→ Natalie I'll pray for you.

Tyson, however, did not pray for her. At least
not yet. Instead he looked at Stefan's message again.
And again. Then he answered:

→ Who are you?

Stefan's reply was instant.

→ Help me. Help me!

Was this some joke? Somehow Tyson didn't think it was.

→ Tell me who you are. And tell me what help you need.

The answer again was super-quick and just as strange.

→ I don't know from where you speak, or how. But I was sending my prayer to my Lord in heaven, and you answered me.

This was getting eerie.

→ Please just explain to me where you are and who you are. And why you need help.

This guy Stefan seemed like he was from another world. His next words reinforced that perception.

→ I am Stefan son of Dedrick of Blue Mountain in Loudriana. But I am now at Gronza at the school of Brother Brendan, in the old fortress. I'm trapped in the top of the bell tower. Who are you? Are you an angel?

Wow, this is actually kind of cool, Tyson thought. Although he had no idea where Loudriana was. It sounded European maybe. But geography was never his strength.

Tyson kept the interchange going:

→ Sorry, no angel here. My name is Tyson Vasser.

→ Then tell me, Tyson Vasser—are you a servant of Jesus, the Lord Christ?

→ Yes I'm a Christian. Tell me Stefan do you actually have a computer in that bell tower?

It took quite a while for Stefan's next reply, which was really surprising to Tyson, since it was only four words:

→ What is a computer?

Interesting. Totally weird, but interesting. Maybe the connection was getting through on Stefan's cell phone or PDA or something.

→ Stefan how are you getting my message?

Another pause.

→ With my ears. As I would hear anyone's voice. Your words ring softly from out of the bell, though I know not how.

Tyson felt a chill. From the pile of clothes on his bed he grabbed a wrinkled Pittsburgh Steelers jersey and pulled it over his T-shirt.

→ So—right now you hear my voice asking you if you can hear me?

Stefan answered quickly:

→ Yes, I can hear you. I was praying for help, and looking upward to heaven, here under the rim of this great bell. Suddenly your voice came to me from out of the bell's heart and mouth. Like a miracle! So tell me, Brother Tyson: If you are not an angel, how can you hear my voice as I speak into the bell?

A bell? This couldn't be. What was happening?

→ But Stefan I'm NOT hearing your voice. I'm seeing your WORDS. I'm reading your words on my computer and—

Tyson jumped up restlessly from his chair. He walked a few steps in a circle, then sat down again and typed fast.

Listen Stefan I'm not understanding this at all. I need you to explain it to me from the beginning.

Fortunately at this moment he remembered some stuff he learned in English class that morning. All about the simple questions to ask when you're investigating something. He continued his instructions to Stefan:

Just give me the straight facts Stefan.
The who, what, when, where, and why.
And the how. Tell me everything. Please.

Tyson pressed the edges of his keyboard with his palms while he waited.

> → Everything, yes, Brother Tyson. I will tell you all that you ask of me. And I hope you receive my words clearly, for I cannot speak loudly here because of our danger.
>
> As for the Who, this I told you already. Also the Where. I am Stefan, and I am in the bell tower of Brother Brendan's school in the old fortress at Gronza, in Loudriana, in the foothills of the Alps.

Tyson interrupted:

> → In Europe?

In the seconds before the answer came through, he sensed Stefan's frustration.

> → Of course Europe.
>
> Also with me here is a young girl who is badly hurt. She is Juliana, Brother Brendan's daughter.

You also asked me for the What. The What is simple and harsh. We are alone and trapped here because of Marmeccan raiders from the mountains. I heard them say they will burn this tower and everything around us at daybreak. But they are not aware we are here. And I've prayed in agony to the Lord because I do not know what to do.

And as for the When…surely you know it already: This is the evening of the tenth day of the tenth month. In the year of our Lord one thousand and six.

Tyson read over those last couple of sentences about a half dozen times. Finally he tapped out this request:

→ Please tell me that last part again Stefan. Just the date.

Another impatient pause.

→ The date is no mystery. Why do you say you do not know it? But what does it matter anyway? Brother Tyson, why do you ask

me questions instead of helping me? Why
do you torment me in my hour of need?

Tyson shot back:

→ Wait Stefan, wait. Please don't get upset.
Actually the date really is a mystery. To me
anyway. Where I am this is October 10 in the
year 2006. And if I read you right you're saying
that where you are it's exactly one thousand
years ago. Makes no sense. I don't understand.

There was another long pause. Questions were
bouncing and banging in Tyson's mind.
Then Stefan replied:

→ Brother Tyson, it is I who do not understand. And it is I who now ask for an explanation. What are you trying to say?

Tyson ran his fingers through his hair as his mind
tried sorting this out. He started typing again:

→ It's simple. Where I am, this is the 21st
century and I'm in America and—

But really it wasn't simple, was it? While Tyson was faltering, Stefan filled in the pause:

→ What is America?

Oh yeah. No such thing as America a thousand years ago. *This is so wild*, Tyson was thinking. *And so frustrating*. What was the use of going on?

Stefan came through again:

I dare not trust you, Tyson! What is America? Is it the place of devils? Is it the region of darkness? Do you address me from hell? I fear you are a demon. Answer me, Tyson: Are you a demon? Why are you tormenting me? You are my enemy!

Reading this, Tyson shook his head. "*No!*" he cried aloud, as the words from Stefan kept pouring in:

Why do I cry to my God for help, and you block my way, whoever you are? Why? We are trapped in this place, with nowhere to go, and you use this bell to mock me. *Why?*

Tyson, I will speak to you no longer. Juliana is
stirring in her pain, and I must go to her side
and keep her from groaning too loudly and
revealing our presence to the raiders. I will
speak with you never again, nor will I listen
to you. In the name of the Lord I command
you: *Be silent!*

Tyson couldn't type anything else anyway. He only
wanted to yell or scream or throw something. He sat
staring at these messages, rereading Stefan's words.

There was a knock at his bedroom door.

"Yeah?"

His dad walked in. "Tyson?"

It was a relief to see his dad and hear his voice.
It was like coming back into the real world. Tyson
leaned back in his chair.

"Yeah, Dad?"

"I thought I heard you shout," his father said.
"You okay?"

"I'm fine, Dad. Sorry I woke you."

"Oh, no, you didn't wake me. I was—I was actually in the bathroom, just praying for you."

"You were?" Tyson realized then that his dad was still in his sweatshirt and jeans.

"Yeah, and…and I was praying for lots of things. Even for that report you're working on tonight. Then I got this crazy idea for something you could write about. It just got stuck in my brain. So—unless you're already down the road on something else, do you want to hear the idea?"

"Of course."

"Well—here it is: A *bell*."

Tyson dropped his jaw. He didn't know what to say.

As the silence got awkward, his dad said, "Well, I— I know it's not the best idea in the world. But I wonder: Have bells changed all that much over the centuries? And like I say, the idea just stuck in my mind, so I thought I might as well—"

"No, Dad, it's a great idea. In fact, you won't believe this, but a bell is exactly what's been stuck on my mind too, even when you walked in that door."

"Really? Whoa, how about that." His dad was all smiles. "You didn't need my help after all."

"No, Dad, that's great. You just confirmed it for me. Thanks for telling me."

"You bet. Well, I'm off to bed for real this time. Hope you're not up too late."

"Thanks, Dad."

"Love you, bud. Good night." He closed the door.

Tyson wondered, *How totally weird could one night possibly get?* Maybe he should bury himself under his bedcovers and not come out tomorrow till noon.

But then he looked at his screen and saw more messages from both Jared and Natalie, which he quickly read over. Tonight had now officially gone way beyond weird.

God, he thought. And it was a real prayer. *Help me.*

Here's what Jared told him:

→ tyson i blew it huge. i told you i couldnt talk with my mom tonight i just went on upstairs after she started crying again about scott. i didnt stay down there with her to eat or anything i just walked away and then i heard her still crying. then next thing i know i hear her going out the front door and thought i should check. i didnt here her car, its still parked she didnt take it, so, i went outside and called and called her name. she just ran off i have no idea where.

she hasnt pulled this before, tho shes done plenty of other crazy things because for a long time she has had psycological disorders, but she has never just gone and run off like this and its my falt for not listening and being there for her. should i call 911 and report a missing person. i tryed calling your cell

phone to ask you but you didnt answer.
i checked at our closest neihgbors but Mom
wasnt there ether. i will never forgive myself
if she gets hurt out there or something happens. i thoght i may just get the car and go
driving to look for her myself but cant even
find her car keys. everything goes bad to
worse. tyson please answer. i have never felt
so awful in my life. :-[

Tyson answered, and they exchanged these words:

→ Sorry Jared about my cell phone, it's not
working since I accidentally ran it through
the washer. Think hard Jared. Couldn't your
mom just have walked over to that 7-11
down the street? Why don't you walk down
there and check?

→ good sujestion tyson but mom would
never walk alone at night to 7 11. she always
sends me there if she needs stuff. but maybe
i should at least check it out.

→ You're right Jared it can't hurt. Walk
down there why don't you, then let me

know as soon as you're back. I'm sure your mom's okay wherever she is. If not at 7-11 then keep thinking hard where else she might have gone. Let me know all your ideas when you're back. You can catch me here anytime. Still got that report to write. Could take a long while.

Hey Jared—I'll be praying.

But Tyson didn't pray. Not yet. He turned to Natalie's message:

→ Tyson, I feel there's no one else I can talk with right now. Thank you for the way you're always willing to listen to others…I hear so many people say that about you. I know you've always had a smile and a friendly word for me, but we've never really talked that much. Now I desperately need it.

Tyson, I told you Adam is in trouble. He thinks he should get away fast. Like tonight. And he's saying he has to take me, but I don't want to go. It's almost kidnapping.

You said I had your prayers Tyson. Now I need them more than ever. Will you let me explain why? :-/

Tyson told her yes. And she gave him her story.

Natalie said she had hated home life for a long time, but things were getting unbelievably worse. Natalie and Adam right now were on their own for a few nights, because their mother was living in Pittsburgh and their father was out of town on business until the weekend.

This afternoon, Natalie had left school with a friend of hers from the choir. Natalie didn't expect to return home till after the choir performance at the freshmen parents' program. But she had left her music folder at home, so while her friend's mother was running errands late in the afternoon, she dropped Natalie by her house to retrieve the folder.

➔ Adam didn't hear me slip in. He was with a couple other guys back in his room. I found my folder where I'd left it on the kitchen table this morning, but I overheard these guys talking in the back. For some reason I couldn't stop listening, even though they were saying stuff that made no sense to me. They said they needed to be on good behavior now and not do anything suspicious or draw any attention. They were bragging about the guns they had, but I didn't think Adam owned a gun. And they mentioned a fire. Suddenly I realized what they were talking about.

Tyson, did you hear about the house that burned over the weekend on Camden? My brother and those other two guys— they set that house on fire after they stole some stuff there.

I know this for a fact because suddenly one of the guys came to get something from the kitchen while I stood there, and I couldn't slip away. So then my brother and the other guy stepped in too, and they all confronted me about what I had heard. There was no hiding it. They know I know.

They threatened me if I ever told anyone.
They said it would be worse than hell for
me if I did. They told me I would have to lie
for them if anybody ever tried to question
me about all this.

Tyson I don't know how I could ever keep
going like that. I've never been good at cov-
ering up. If I try, people can always tell I'm
hiding something. :Q

Tyson asked her where Adam was now. Natalie
said her brother had gone to fill his car with gas—

→ and who knows where else? A lot of
times he leaves home just to get by himself.
But I think he'll be back soon. Tonight when
we got home, before he stormed out, he
kept saying he'll have to take me away.
He seemed pretty strong about it.

Tyson asked where Adam was planning to run to.

→ He said Pittsburgh. To Mom's place. He
wants to drive up there tonight and try to
live with her for a while.

It didn't sound like a smart plan. Besides, Tyson told Natalie, the police already knew the fire was arson. If they ever started suspecting Adam, they would suspect him even more if they found out he had skipped town.

➔ You're right Tyson. But Adam's mind is so panicky right now he can't think straight. He and those guys decided today they needed to be on good behavior, like when Adam agreed to give you and Jared a ride. But then his panic gets the best of him and he does stupid things like snap at you and totally lose it on the way home.

Tyson asked why she thought Adam got involved in something this bad.

➔ I don't know. I still can't believe it. He's never been in this kind of trouble before, until he got mixed up with the wrong friends. He told me they never meant for things to go as far as they did last Sunday at that house. Adam just got caught up in all of it, and it spun out of control.

Now he's so afraid, because he told me
tonight that one of the guys has had trouble
with the law before. And if the police suspect this guy and corner him about the fire,
Adam's sure the guy will squeal on him. :(

Tyson thought it might be wise if Natalie phoned
her dad or mom and got their help. He suggested this
to Natalie.

→ No, Adam made me swear not to. But
Tyson—I want to give you the phone number
where my dad is. If anything happens to me
please call him.

She gave him a phone number for a hotel in
Wilmington, Delaware.

→ Natalie shouldn't I go ahead and phone
him now, and get your dad in on all this? It's
getting scary.

→ Yes it's scary, believe me Tyson I know.
But please don't phone anybody yet,
because I promised Adam I wouldn't.

→ Okay I won't. But Natalie if you change your mind let me know anytime, cause I'll be right here. A super-late night for me— big history report due tomorrow and I haven't even started.

There was a pause, then this from Natalie:

→ I just heard Adam coming in. He's back. Got to go. :-S

Tyson rose from the desk and laid on his back on the bed, without bothering to move the clothes spread all over it. He stared up at a poster on his ceiling, a picture of mountain bikers riding over massive reddish-brown rock slopes out west. His uncle in Denver had sent him the poster after inviting Tyson out west someday to go mountain biking at a place called Moab in Utah. The photograph showed a trail in Moab called Slickrock.

"What do I do now, God?" he said aloud, though he was feeling that God was even further away than Slickrock Trail. Tyson was tired, he was confused, and something inside seemed to give him even more pain than his injured ribs.

A part of his mind was like an icebreaker ship in a frozen polar sea, pushing and crashing forward to make a breakthrough for his friends. But another part of him wished he'd never even heard about Jared's and Natalie's problems. He felt almost like running away somewhere himself.

He rubbed his side again as he stared upward at the poster, his eyes following the sweep of the slopes and ledges and rocky towers in the picture. Silently, he tried a prayer once more. *O God, give us some help. To Natalie and Jared. And to me.*

Tyson got up and returned to the desk, wondering if Jared had made it back home after checking at the corner store for his mom.

He found a message on his screen, but it wasn't from Jared.

> → Brother Tyson! If you are there, I would speak with you again. This is Stefan.

Oh no, Tyson thought. This was definitely not what he needed right now. If it wasn't for staying in touch with Jared and Natalie, he would just shut down the computer altogether and forget this other guy.

But Stefan came through again.

Brother Tyson?

He might as well answer.

> → Hello again Stefan. This is Tyson.

→ Ah! Brother Tyson, thank you for answering. I have been praying, so now my mind is clearer than before. I was wrong to be so disturbed with you. I was wrong to accuse you of being a demon and my enemy and my tormenter. Will you forgive me for these offenses?

→ Yes Stefan I forgive you.

→ You are not a demon, are you? You are neither angel nor demon.

→ Yes Stefan that's right. I'm neither one. Never have been. Never will be.

→ And all that you have told me is true? Though it seems so utterly impossible to me?

→ Yes. I didn't lie to you Stefan.

→ So you, Brother Tyson, are living a thousand years in this world's future?

→ Well it's not the future to me. It's the present. But you're living a thousand years in the past. At least it sounds that way to me.

→ A thousand years, yes! But this is no matter, Brother Tyson. The Lord has reminded me of his words in the Great Book: With the Lord, a day is as a thousand years, and a thousand years is as a day. So I see that even one thousand years is no impossible distance. After all, it is already a wonder that your voice speaks to me from this bell; if such a thing can happen, then certainly your voice can also circle back from far down the pathway of time. Nothing is too difficult for the Lord—the Great Book says so.

→ Yeah that's right Stefan. I remember that verse.

A sudden thought jolted Tyson.

Hey Stefan, by the way—how did you come to speak such good modern English?

→ What is it you said?

→ I mean—what language exactly are you speaking, Stefan?

→ Of course I speak the German dialect of Loudriana, the same as you are. Why do you ask? Would you rather we spoke in Latin?

→ No. It's nothing Stefan. Forget I asked.

So that bell even did the translation work. Incredible. Tyson was realizing he could never explain this to his friends. They would never believe him.

Stefan kept up his questioning:

→ You said before, Brother Tyson, that you are not listening to my words, but rather reading them. Are they appearing to you like the handwriting on the wall in the days of Daniel?

→ No, not like that exactly. But—it's too complicated to explain really.

→ And the place where you are, Tyson—I suppose it is not in Europe. What did you call the place?

→ America. And no, it isn't in Europe.

→ Then it is somewhere in Asia?

→ No.

→ In Africa?

→ No. It's far
across the ocean
from all those places. I
wish I could explain it,
Stefan, so you understood. But this is all so
incredibly strange.

→ Yes it is, Brother Tyson, but I do not
believe the Lord means it to be so.
Therefore we now face together one
supreme question.

→ We do? What's that?

→ It is this: Why has the Lord bound us
together in such a way? And surely the
answer is not a mystery. You *can* help me,
Brother Tyson.

→ How?

→ In one way only, I now believe. But it is the best and greatest way. You can *pray* for me, brother. Because I truly see no way to escape these Marmeccan raiders—and no way out alive from this tower.

→ Yeah. I could pray, Stefan.

→ Brother Tyson, a moment ago I was remembering the wonderful psalm that Solomon wrote in the Great Book, a psalm about the noble and righteous man. Solomon said this about him: "May prayer be made for him always, and may blessings be spoken for him all the day." And now, my brother, from you I have learned that this word *always* means even to a thousand years! In God's eyes, "all the day" can be ten centuries long! I wonder if you, my brother, are called across those centuries to look back and pray for me and speak blessings for me in this my night of danger. Will you do this, my brother?

Tyson wanted to say yes. But he was reminded just then of the sloppy way he kept his promises to pray for Natalie and for Jared, not to mention other people he should be praying for. He felt so far behind in all this praying. It didn't seem wise to add any more obligations.

→ Are you still there, Brother Tyson?

This was getting irritating actually. And he wished this guy would break off this "Brother Tyson" stuff.

→ Yes Stefan I'm still here. And you don't have to call me Brother.

A long pause.

→ You are not willing to pray for me, are you?

Tyson felt bad. He could almost sense the tears forming in Stefan's eyes. He struggled with how to answer.

Tyson, are you there?

→ Yes I'm here. The fact is Stefan, this is not an easy time for me either. I'm way behind in praying for lots of people. So it seems stupid to promise to pray for you when really I'm not sure I would ever get around to it.

Another slow and silent lull.

→ Tyson, I should never demand anything from you. If my request has been a burden to you, I ask for your pardon.

→ No, no, Stefan, you were right to ask. I respect you for it. Honestly.

→ Then it seems, Tyson, that we return again to the vital question: Why has the Lord brought us together in this urgent moment? If the answer that I had imagined is wrong, then tell me: What is *your* answer? Why are our voices connecting across the centuries, across this canyon of time that is no obstacle to God? Why has the Sovereign and Mighty Lord allowed this bell to carry our human words into each other's presence in this my darkest of nights?

Tyson had no answer. Then a new thought staggered his mind: Maybe this freaky connection to the past was meant to somehow allow Tyson to alter the course of history. To literally change the world. Or did God just want to change *Tyson's* world—and use this stranger Stefan to do it?

Then Tyson's mind sank to something closer to home. It was that history report due tomorrow. He looked at his alarm clock. It was past eleven, and he still hadn't started it. But the strange idea came to him of how rad it would be to have a lot of first-hand information from Stefan about bells—some actual, accurate research from a thousand years ago. That could be impressive stuff to Mr. Miller. It could definitely boost his history grade.

→ Have you gone, Tyson?

→ No Stefan I'm here. I was thinking.
Actually, I don't really know the answer to
why we're talking. This whole thing blows
my mind. But here's what I'm wondering.
Why don't you tell me more about yourself,
and where you are and all, what it's like.

Do you have time to do that? I could actually pray for you better—that is, if the time comes when I CAN pray—if I know more about you. So tell me what it's like there. Look around you in that tower. Look up into that bell. What's it like?

The pause here was the longest yet.

→ I will be honest with you, Tyson, as you have been honest. To me, you seem more curious than kind. More selfish than serving. But I do not mind telling you more of my circumstances here. Though you make no commitment to me on this dark night, I will tell you my story, even if it be the last account I shall ever give to anyone here on this earth.

Tyson followed the words as the stranger told his story.

Stefan stated again that he was from a place called Blue Mountain, in the region called Loudriana. His father Dedrick was a nobleman in the court of the duke of Loudriana; the duke in turn was a servant to Henry II, the king of all the Saxons and the holy emperor of the Reich.

Stefan said he was in his fifteenth autumn of life. Tyson interrupted him:

→ Hey, that's the same as me. I turn 15 next month.

→ Then Tyson, are you also in training as a knight, as I am?

→ A knight! No, not me. But YOU are? That's wild. Tell me everything about it.

As a boy, Stefan had left home in his seventh year and was sent to the royal city of Bamberg to become a page. He learned honor, hunting, courtly manners, and the basics of military strategy. He was also under the tutorship of Brother Brendan, a man of God and a warrior in prayer. Brendan soaked the boy's mind in the Scriptures. He taught Stefan, in all his actions, to pursue wisdom, justice, courage, and self-control.

But inside himself, Stefan came to see that those virtues were all alien to his soul. He could not hide the truth that his heart and mind were sick with self-ishness and evil.

As Stefan despaired, Brother Brendan wisely turned his mind and heart to the Great Book. And to the good news it told. Jesus, the pure and only Son of God the Father, had come and walked the ground of this earth. And to pay the punishment for Stefan's evil, he had been killed on an ugly cross. But death could not keep him. Jesus was alive, to bring deliverance to anyone who looked to him for it.

Stefan's soul took hold of this news. His heart flew up with joy like a bird released from a cage. In the wide and rushing waters of the Rednitz River, where fish were leaping, Brother Brendan baptized Stefan on an Easter afternoon.

Meanwhile, his training continued. A year ago, Stefan had been appointed a squire to the knight Karlik of Bamberg. Besides learning combat, Stefan spent his days cleaning his master's armor, preserving his

weapons, tending his horse, and consuming his stories.

Then word came to Bamberg of trouble in the south of Loudriana. A small pagan tribe from the east, known as Marmeccans, had moved into the mountain forests. They were launching raids into the towns and villages below, burning and plundering. This was a special concern to Stefan, because his former tutor, Brother Brendan, was now a teacher at a school in the area where the raiders were attacking.

King Henry asked Karlik to take a band of warriors and ride south to put an end to this Marmeccan threat. As his squire, Stefan's duty was to ride beside

Sir Karlik and never abandon him in battle. This would be Stefan's first taste of fighting.

As they drew near, they learned that the most threatened area was the town of Balantiere. This was only an hour's ride from where Brother Brendan had moved his school into the old hillside fortress of Gronza. While the warriors made their headquarters in Balantiere and prepared to fight from there, Sir Karlik asked Stefan to ride to Gronza and to bring back Brother Brendan and any others from the school who could fight. "I must have Brendan here," Sir Karlik said, "for reasons of my own. Let nothing stop him from coming. And assist him in whatever way you can."

Stefan obeyed. He rode alone to the old fortress and was thrilled to be reunited with Brother Brendan. He discovered that all the younger boys in the school had been taken away a few weeks earlier, for their safety. All the servants were gone as well. Only the older boys were left, plus Brother Brendan's ten-year-old daughter, Juliana.

Stefan dutifully passed along to Brendan his master's orders to evacuate and join the warriors at Balantiere. But this brought a crisis.

That same day, in the same hour as Stefan's arrival, Juliana had fallen from a horse. She fell because she had been foolishly riding while she was ill. Now, to add to her rising fever, she had a splintered leg bone, which Brendan did not feel capable to set. Her leg was rapidly swelling.

"Someone must stay with Juliana until we can send a healer from Balantiere," Brendan said. "But Sir Karlik orders me away. I ask you, Stefan: Will you stay with my daughter until we can send back help?"

Stefan's heart quivered. It would likely be well into daylight tomorrow before anyone returned, and he couldn't bear the possibility of missing the coming battle. Besides, did he not have a duty to return to his master's side? But he saw no escape from agreeing to Brendan's request.

"I will do as you think best, Brother Brendan." But in his heart he rebuked this girl-child for her foolishness and for what it was costing him.

To make matters worse, the fever began to frenzy Juliana's mind. When she heard that her father must leave her to prepare for battle, she wailed that the raiders would surely come here to Gronza and kill her, and she couldn't run away from them. She had no trust in her guardian, this stranger Stefan.

There were caves hidden in the nearby hillsides, and Brendan asked the boys from the school to take his daughter inside one of them where she might feel safer. They carried her there on a board covered with a straw mat. The school's pet dog, a spotted brown and white hound that the boys called Otto, followed dutifully at their heals. But when they laid Juliana in the cavern, she cried out that she couldn't bear the cold, damp dreariness. They built a fire, but she refused to be comforted, and screamed even more.

"She seems nearly out of her mind," Brendan lamented to Stefan. "How can I leave her this way? But with every passing moment, we risk Sir Karlik's wrath if we delay any longer."

Then one of the boys suggested that they move the girl into the top of the old fortress tower, to the landing where the warning bell hung. It was bright and airy there, nothing like the cavern. And it was probably just as safe. Perhaps this would give Juliana peace of mind.

Whether it would or not, Brendan was determined that this must be where his daughter would stay.

They carried her back to the fortress, then hitched ropes to her straw-matted board and hauled her up onto the landing inside the bell tower's top.

Juliana lay tossing and turning on her mat as her father gave her a hurried goodbye. "Don't be afraid," Brendan whispered as he bent over her. "There's no reason the attackers would come here anyway. All we have at Gronza are parchments and school slates, which raiders don't care for, and a few scrawny animals that are hardly worth the taking. So you'll be safe here, I promise. Stefan will make sure of it."

There was a basin of cool water beside her, and Brendan dipped a cloth in it and wiped her face. It was all he knew to do for his daughter's illness.

Brendan stood and clapped his hand on Stefan's shoulder, then hurried down the ladder.

From inside the tower's top, Stefan leaned his arms on the timber railing above the half-wall that enclosed the bell landing. With a sinking heart, he watched below as Brendan and the boys rode out through the gateway and down the Balantiere road. Below him, in the cobbled courtyard beneath the bell tower, Otto the hound watched everyone leave as well, and he looked just as sad as Stefan felt.

Then Stefan set himself to the task of bringing up a store of food and water for Juliana. With two full water buckets in each hand, he counted forty-five steps on the creaky wooden stairs winding up along the tower's outer wall, plus seven more on the ladder that went through an opening in the landing floor. Fifty-two steps altogether.

On the next trip he brought up two baskets of bread and apples and burnt bacon and cheese and candles. On the next he took blankets to cover her when the cool of the evening came. On his last climb, he carried up a few books he had selected from the schoolroom. Juliana was sleeping more quietly now, and there was still an hour of daylight left. He would sit beside her and read while he could.

The book he opened first was a collection of someone's contemplations from the Gospel of John. This was to Stefan's liking. Years ago, while he was first learning the Scriptures from Brother Brendan, Stefan had made the prayer life of Jesus his special study and reflection. He had quickly discovered that nothing was better for this than John's Gospel.

Reading these pages brought back to Stefan's mind those days of countless discoveries under Brendan's teaching.

In the midst of those years, he spent one winter's day observing a falconer training his hunting birds. More than any other time before or since, Stefan had kept his eye to the sky through the whole of that day. He had sensed indescribable beauty in the blueness and in the changing sweep and layering of clouds. He had felt closer to God than ever before.

Throughout that day he thought of the man Jesus walking this same earth beneath this same sky. He thought of Jesus looking up, in the midst of his busy ministry, to talk with his Father in heaven, hour after hour. Stefan ached with longing to pray this way. But he felt so far from being able to do it.

That evening, kneeling beside the firelight, he made a vow to the Lord to pursue this goal in his life: to pray as Jesus prayed. Since then, he had learned so much.

In the quietness of the bell tower, Stefan slowly read his book as Juliana slept, while Otto wandered the deserted spaces below. The sun went down, firing the western sky with red-golden streaks. Then the day's light began to fade. Soon he would need a candle if he wanted to keep reading.

He reached over to feel Juliana's forehead, which was still feverishly hot. He dipped the cloth in the water and wiped her face. She kept her eyes closed. He was thankful for the rest she was finding. He was pierced in his heart for the bitter complaints he had inwardly muttered because of her fall. He asked for God's forgiveness, and he prayed for her healing and comfort.

Then he stood and stretched his arms. In that moment, he saw them—the raiders approaching on horseback on the path leading down from the forest heights. Hurriedly Stefan crouched down to avoid being seen. He had spotted four of them.

He quietly went to the opening in the floor of the landing, pulled up the ladder, then gently shut the trapdoor over the hole.

By this time, Otto was barking at the intruders. Through a few cracks in the half-wall around the landing, Stefan watched one of the men approach the dog and slash it with his sword. Otto let out a dying yelp. Then the raiders walked around the old fortress, entering doors to rummage in the rooms. One of the men went into the swineyard and stabbed a pig, then dragged it into the courtyard, where he built a roasting fire.

Stefan heard the men talking in their native tongue, but to one of the men—perhaps a captured slave, or more likely their spy—they spoke in German. That's why Stefan was able to overhear their plans. They did not care for this place, and were disappointed in having found nothing of value inside the buildings. They spoke of having seen an ugly iron cross hanging on a wall inside one room, and one man wondered if it carried some curse.

Since darkness was settling, they decided to feast on the pig for the night. They would make another search in the morning. After that, they would burn the buildings, kill the rest of the swine and the few goats and chickens, and leave the place a ruin.

"And now," Stefan said, "these four have finished their pork dinners in the courtyard. They still ring the roaring fire. They joke and swear and belch and nervously laugh. They glance guardedly into the darkness around them. And they look to the coming day to burn and to destroy."

While Stefan was telling this story, Tyson heard details that were so much like the daydreams he'd known throughout his boyhood, when he imagined himself alive in the days of knights and chivalry. In a way, it was hard to sense Stefan's real danger, because surely there had to be a way of escape for him. Wasn't that always true for the hero in the old stories?

Tonight Tyson found himself present as never before in those centuries past, through all that Stefan was sharing with him. Would there be a happy ending to this episode? There had to be. And helping Stefan find it was almost a game for Tyson.

→ Stefan, do you have weapons with you?

→ I carry a dagger, and I have a staff.

→ Well, while those guys are down there stuffed and groggy from their dinner, couldn't you slip down the tower, sneak up on them from behind, and overpower them before they realize what's happening?

→ But Tyson, right now, the men are two facing two. And they are watchful. For me to come behind one pair would be to come face-to-face with the other. There would be no surprise.

→ Then what about later tonight, Stefan, when they slumber off? It ought to be fairly easy to clobber them then, shouldn't it?

→ Yes, Tyson, overcoming them later might indeed be less difficult. And if I were now alone in this tower, I might just venture such a thing, even for the sport of it. But I am not alone. I have Juliana in my charge. If I failed to take down all four of those men, or if I myself were injured or captured or killed, I cannot count on those barbarians to show her any mercy. I would have failed to pro-tect her. And I cannot risk that.

Tyson thought some more.

→ Then what about the two of you just creeping out and escaping into the woods?

→ No, we could not. Juliana has broken bones and a raging fever. She could travel only painfully, and her mind is so distraught that I am fearful I could not prevent her from crying out.

→ Couldn't you leave her by herself just long enough for you to ride away and bring back help?

→ No, Tyson, I will not leave her. To find herself alone would make her wild with fear.

→ Well then—could you maybe take her along with you if you drugged her first? Or knocked her unconscious?

The instant Tyson finished typing that last sugges-tion, he realized it wasn't the right one.

That was definitely Stefan's view as well:

→ Tyson, that is unspeakable! My duty is to

protect her! Has all chivalry died out in the thousand years between me and you?

Well, most of it probably has. But Tyson decided not to go there.

→ I hear you Stefan. I was just exploring options. There's got to be some way out of this for you both, and I want to help you find it.

→ Tyson, I have already requested the help I truly need from you.

→ You have? Oh yeah, you have. To pray for you. But is that all? Is that really the only thing I can do?

→ *All? Only?* Tyson, has faith in the living God also died out in the thousand years between me and you?

Well—maybe that too, Tyson figured. *To some extent anyway.* But then he thought more seriously.

No! There had to be a good reason for this crazy, mysterious connection he was having with Stefan.

God had a purpose in it. Tyson had to believe that. He had to fight for Stefan somehow, and he had to do it God's way.

If only he really knew how.

Tyson? Are you still there, Tyson?

→ Yes Stefan I'm here. And I want to tell you something. I WILL pray for you. I make that commitment. But I also have a request.

→ What is it, my brother?

→ The fact is, Stefan—to be honest, I hardly even know HOW to pray. But you're an expert. And I want to pray as you do—the way Jesus prayed. Stefan, will you teach me how?

PART TWO

BEFORE
THE
DAWN

12:16 A.M.

Stefan told Tyson he was stepping over to comfort Juliana. She was getting restless again.

While Tyson waited for Stefan's return, he found a message from Jared. Jared was back home and had some news.

> → so tyson heres what i found out. mom was there at 7 11 all right. the guy there remembered her. he said she walked in and was carrying a flashlight and she bougt a packet of emergncey candles plus the guy gave her a book of matches which she asked for too then she walked out. however the guy didnt notise which way she went but did say he thoght she was walking not driving because he couldnt remember a car pulling away at the time. but anyway she didnt come home with those candles because she isnt here she went somewhere else.

This was good, Tyson thought—some news was better than no news, even if it still didn't tell them exactly where Jared's mom was.

They talked about it:

→ So, Jared, where do you think she might have gone with those candles? To church maybe?

→ Maybe to a church but i dont know. are churchs open this late its already past midnite.

→ I think some are, some aren't. But I think it's a good chance that a church is where she's at. I bet she was just wanting to pray. What do you think? Sometimes candles can help you get quiet and concentrate if you want to talk with God. I even keep one here in my room that I light sometimes.

→ good for you i guess. but mom doesnt go much to church. besides do you have to take your own candles when you go there. this is all strange and i just dont know. should i call 9 1 1 what do you think? :-Q

Tyson couldn't say.

→ Jared if you feel you should call 911 go ahead and call. I guess it can't hurt. Did the guy at the store say anything about how your mom looked? Like did she seem really upset or nervous or anything?

→ he only said she was pretty quiet which i guess is not bad

→ I think you're right Jared, I think that's good. You know, maybe your mom just needed to step out and get some fresh air, which can help a lot sometimes. Maybe you should expect her to need times like that. Give her some space. It probably takes a while to work through grief before you finally learn that losing someone is not the end of the world.

It took a while for Jared to reply.

→ easy for you to say tyson but you know it really was the end of the world for scott.

And it was the end of the world for what
our famly once had and for what we used
to be. :-[

Tyson inwardly scolded himself for being insensitive.

→ Jared, I'm sorry. I wasn't thinking straight.

→ no tyson i think maybe its just that you
have never been in our shoes and so how
can you know what its like. scott was always
the center of everything for us he was moms

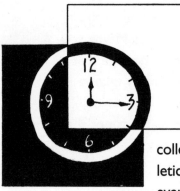

hope she even called
him that. and he was
my hero in a lot of
ways. scott had
everything going for
him he was smart
and going to finish
college and he was so ath-
letic and good looking and
everybody liked him. he
wasn't like me with so many falts and failuers.
scott was everything to us and everything to
me because i have never known or even seen
my dad. he was a miner and died in a mine

collapse when i was only 2. and now scott is also gone. i still cant believe it and when i get to where i finaly am believing it then it just hurts even more. like a knife stabbing me inside. i hate it. i hate this so bad and it makes me hate god too and now ive hurt my mom and i cant even be a freind to her when she needs me more than ever. she has lost her hope and i can never fill that place for her. no one can. least of all me. so tyson just lite that candle of yours and talk with god if you want to but so far it isnt helping. :-\

Tyson felt like he'd been hit in the face with a slap he probably deserved.

→ What can I say Jared? You're right. So what now? What are you going to do?

But Jared wasn't answering. Tyson might as well have been asking himself: *What now?*

Then Natalie came through again.

→ Tyson, Adam and I just had a really hard talk. He was saying again that I will have to go away with him. I kept telling him I can't, but when it comes down to it I guess I'm afraid to resist too hard because I just don't know what he might do. He kept saying I have to do this for his sake.

And Tyson, there's something else I have to tell you. Maybe I made a mistake in this, but I just didn't know what else to do, so I finally went ahead and told Adam that you know all about him setting the fire and all, because I told you. So their crime isn't secret anymore. I thought it might help if Adam knew this. I even told him that your dad works for the government. :-[

Tyson couldn't believe what he was reading.

→ Natalie are you crazy? Besides it's the post office my dad works for, and what could THEY do? Put Adam's picture up in the lobby?

→ But Tyson, I was desperate. I've got to stop Adam somehow. I don't want to see him and his friends going weird and forcing

me to go away with them. You don't understand how scary this is for me. Telling Adam
about you may not have been the wisest
thing to do but I had to try something.

→ So what did Adam say when you told him?

→ He was just totally silent for a long while
but that was the scary part. When Adam
gets the most angry or afraid he doesn't yell
at people, he just goes totally silent and
then later he explodes with action. I thought
he might even punch me or throw something at me. But this time he just stalked out
the door, right after he told me again to be
ready to leave with him when he gets back.

→ Natalie, do you think he's coming over
HERE?

→ Well…it's the first thought that came to
my mind Tyson. But I don't know. Adam's
mind is so shaky and spooked right now,
I don't know what he'll try. :-Q

Tyson wondered what he would do if Adam came after him. Adam was twice his size. And what if Adam brought along those other two guys?

→ Natalie why the heck did you tell him about me? That was dumb.

→ Tyson, I'm doing the best I can! You don't know what this is like for me, what pressure this is. So please do NOT expect to be Miss Cool Calm Perfect Judgment right now. :-@

Tyson cringed. He felt he'd only blown it again while trying to help someone.

→ I'm sorry Natalie, please forgive me. I guess I was thinking only of me and forgetting you.

→ Tyson, even if you believe there's nothing you can do to help me...you did say something before about praying. I think I need you to do that for me. Because why would God listen to me?

Tyson brooded over how to answer her question, and stalled. He wanted to say God would listen to Natalie for exactly the same reason he would ever listen to anybody—because they look to God when they know they need his help. But was that right? Tyson couldn't get his thoughts put together before Natalie jumped in and wrapped things up:

→ Tyson, I think I'll go pack a bag, just in case. If I'm not ready to go when Adam gets back it may throw him in a rage. I'll talk to you later. I hope you still have my dad's phone number. Thanks and bye.

Yeah, *thanks and bye,* Tyson thought, while his brain kept spinning. Jared and Natalie: Two people. Two disasters. Too much.

12:54 a.m.

Tyson lit the candle on the shelf above his desk, and turned out his desk lamp. All the other lights in the house were off as well. If Adam drove up, Tyson wanted the place looking dark.

He rested his fingers on his keyboard.

→ Stefan. Stefan are you there?

→ I am here. I am back, Brother Tyson. Oh, I'm sorry—you don't wish me to call you that.

→ Please DO call me that, Stefan. Call me your brother. I realize it's a privilege. So tell me, are the raiders still down there by the fire?

→ They are. They still talk among themselves, and look over their shoulders. And in their uneasiness they keep throwing wood on the fire, so it blazes and crackles—which is good, to help hide any noise that might reach them from up here.

→ And how is Juliana?

→ Her forehead still burns, but she is rest-ing again, and quiet.

→ Stefan, don't you need to get some sleep as well?

→ No, not now, not for me. This is a night for staying awake and staying close to God. Like the times Jesus spent all night in prayer. But perhaps you, Brother Tyson, should be getting rest. Am I keeping you from sleep?

→ No. Some other people are keeping me plenty busy here tonight. Actually they des-perately need prayer. Like I do. And you too of course. Hey Stefan, I'm serious about ask-ing for your help on that. I want to hear all those things you've learned about praying as Jesus prayed. I need a crash course.

→ A crash course? What does that mean?

→ It means you tell me all you can right now, fast. Not waiting for someday later.

After a pause, Stefan said this:

→ For me, Brother Tyson, I cannot count on there being a someday later. I may well have only from now until dawn to live—less than six hours.

→ Stefan don't get discouraged. Don't be thinking that way. It can't be healthy. Just tell me those prayer things.

→ Yes, my brother—a crash course it will be. And I—*Oh no!*

What was that about?

→ Stefan?

There was silence for several minutes, and it worried Tyson. Had the raiders discovered Stefan's presence?

But finally his words returned.

→ I am sorry, Brother Tyson, for the delay. I saw a rat moving across the landing floor toward Juliana. Imagine that, so high up in this tower! It must be a messenger of the devil to make the girl scream. I am very fortunate to have spotted its movement—there's so little light here, with only a three-quarters moon out in the sky tonight, and all is shadowy under the bell tower's roof.

I was trying to kill the rat before it frightened Juliana, but I knew I had to do it quietly. I was just about to pounce on it when I nearly stumbled over Juliana on her mat. I reached up and grabbed the bell's pull-rope, and almost yanked it hard before I let go. *I nearly rang the bell!* That would be the end of our hideout here. I let go of the rope just in time, but the rat got away.

A question gnawed at Tyson's mind as he read this. What else might have happened if the bell had rung? Besides revealing Stefan's location to the raiders—would it also have shut off Tyson's connection with Stefan's voice? Would it be the end of their conversations forever? Tyson wondered.

Stefan kept speaking:

After that, I woke up Juliana to move her mat closer beside me, here under the bell. That way I can still speak with you while I have her close—and I can keep the rats away.

Then I decided to explain to Juliana about the bell and your voice, which seems an awesome wonder to her. She isn't sure whether to believe me. Brother Tyson, will you say something to Juliana, if I can keep her awake a moment longer, so she can hear your voice as I have heard it? But please, not too loudly.

Tyson didn't suppose he had any volume control anyway in this set-up, so he launched into a friendly greeting.

→ Hello, Juliana! This is Tyson Vasser. You've certainly got a good protector there in Stefan, don't you think?

A pause.

Can you hear me, Juliana?

It was Stefan who answered:

→ Yes, Tyson, she can hear you. Clear as a bell.

Funny guy. Stefan's remark sidetracked Tyson's thoughts for a moment. Suddenly he envisioned the first line for his history paper: "For the past thousand years and more, bells have been known for ringing clearly."

Stefan went on:

I fear that your voice has overwhelmed
Juliana with amazement, my brother. But she
is still dazed with pain and weakness from
her illness, and wants only to go back to
sleep. So please pardon her for not speaking
to you.

A few more silent minutes passed. Stefan was probably wiping the girl's face again with the damp rag.

While Tyson waited, he stared into the flickering candle on the shelf above him. *God, help Juliana to get through this. Help Stefan get through it too. Please give them a way out!*

It felt so good and right to be praying for them, even something this simple.

Tyson sensed the pain in his ribs again, but this time it made him thankful that it wasn't a fractured leg he was dealing with, or a dangerous fever.

Stefan returned:

> → Juliana is so tired and weak. Already she
> sleeps again. If later she remembers your
> words to her, I suppose it will be only as a
> dream. O Lord, let her dreams now be
> sweet. Bless Juliana's rest, and heal her. Bring
> her deliverance from this disease. Bring her
> deliverance from the injury to her bones.
> And bring her deliverance from the enemies
> below us. Amen.

"Amen," Tyson said quietly, leaning back in his chair as Stefan began to teach him.

> So, my Brother Tyson, you want to pray as
> Jesus prayed. You have asked me to show
> you what I know of these things.

I believe you are wise to ask for this, Brother Tyson, even if I am no master. Your heart is like that of the disciples of Jesus. For after they saw him praying, they said to him, "Train *us* to pray." So may the Lord himself be your teacher in whatever words I have to say.

I can give you seven special teachings that I have learned about this. I found that it is very easy for me to forget them, so I have trained my mind how to rediscover them again and again.

In the northern sky just beyond the rim of this tower's roof, I can see the seven stars of the Great Dipper. The seven teachings I can show you are like those seven stars in that constellation, which shines so brightly and never fails to point the way to true North for every traveler. When I first see those stars every evening, I follow their line from the outer rim to the handle-point, and each star reminds me of one of those seven lessons.

I come across other reminders as well. Lying beside me, on the landing floor where I am kneeling, is the ladder that brought me up on the final climb into this lofty place. It has seven steps. The seven teachings I can show you are like those seven steps, so good for taking us upward to the highest of high places.

Stefan certainly had a strange way of thinking and speaking. Tyson thought this must be the teaching style Stefan learned from Brother Brendan. It must be how pages and squires were tutored long ago.
Stefan continued:

Brother Tyson, I love these seven teachings. They are surely not the only good lessons on prayer. And for better Christians than I am, they might not even be the most important lessons. But for me, in my days on the earth, they have been loyal friends and faithful guides, always leading me closer to my Lord Jesus.

I am honored to share these seven with you, Brother Tyson, if you agree to hear them.

Tyson quickly agreed.

1:10 A.M.

The first step and first beacon-star that Stefan explained to Tyson was this: To remember that Jesus, in his life on earth, was a *man*. A human being in every way.

Tyson wondered why this was so important.

→ Because, Brother Tyson, if we don't learn to see the humanity of Jesus—to realize that he was genuinely a man—we will never really see him as our true example for *anything*. Instead we will always think in the roots of our mind, "Jesus is God and I am not. And that is why I can never really live in the good way he did."

Tyson's mind had often followed this exact line of thought. It always seemed logical to him.

→ But Stefan, Jesus WAS God and IS God. In fact, come to think of it, why did Jesus even need to pray at all while he was on earth?

→ Exactly the point, Brother Tyson! Jesus *did* pray. He prayed all the time. And he prayed out of his humanity, as a human being who depended on his Father God, just as you and I must depend on God. Jesus prayed as a man to show us how we, as men, must also pray.

→ Okay, I guess I see your point Stefan. Jesus was a total human being, I know that. But I think a lot of people seem to forget the more important fact that he's also God. So it's probably not smart to make such a big deal about him being a man. Besides I've never been able to put those two facts together very well—Jesus as God and Jesus as man. I think it's confusing for most people. We probably need to lean one way or the other before it makes any sense to us, before it's reasonable. And if you ask me, if we have to choose between the two, then I say go with Jesus as God.

→ But Tyson, we should never choose between them! It is wrong to make that choice. Here is a better way I like to think of it: In the Great Book, John tells us that *God is love*. That is a God-fact. Love is a God-fact, a God-reality. And nothing could prove this God-reality to us more than for God to become a man—to show himself to us and to rescue us from our own evil. God is love, and Jesus is God, therefore Jesus became a man to display that love. It is the humanity of Jesus that proves the love. And his perfect love proves in turn that Jesus is God.

Stefan's words were circling around in Tyson's brain and not really coming down for a landing. Tyson figured he was never going to win any theological arguments with a guy this smart. Tyson wanted to get more practical.

→ So Stefan, what difference does this really make in our praying—to remember that Jesus was a man?

→ For myself, Brother Tyson, I have found that unless I remember this teaching, I don't even ask *What would Jesus pray?* I have no reason to ask it. But when my heart remembers that

Jesus was a man just as I am, I never forget
how glad and helpful this question can be.

This led quickly to Stefan's second step,
to his second beacon-star. Stefan expressed
it this way:

→ The story of Jesus is *your*
story; the life of Jesus is *your*
life; his pathway is *your* pathway. You are to follow fully in
his footsteps, just as the Great
Book says: Anyone who is claiming to
live in Jesus must *walk as Jesus walked.*

Tyson felt that this was maybe going too far.

→ But Stefan, I was never born in a manger.
And there's no reason for me to go to
Jerusalem and die on a cross like Jesus did.
He already died for all our sins, didn't he?

→ Yes he did, Tyson—he died once for all as
our ransom. Thank him for this every day.
Thank him that because he died, we have *life.*

But in that life, each of us has our own cross and our own dying to do. Doesn't Jesus tells us to take up *our cross* and *follow him?*

And also in the Great Book, when our brother Paul says, "With Christ I have been crucified," isn't he teaching us to experience the same thing as well? Paul also tells us we are *joined* with Jesus in the likeness of both his death and his resurrection. His cross, his resurrection— everything in the experience of Jesus is a pattern and pathway for my life and for yours.

Tyson still wasn't convinced, but he kept quiet this time.

So now, Tyson, we have looked at two steps on the ladder, two stars in the constellation. Remember these teachings whenever you ask, *What would Jesus pray?* Remember that Jesus was a man as you are a man. And remember that everything in his story is in your story. Therefore everything *he* prayed, *you* can pray. Everything in his prayer life should be in your prayer life as well.

Everything? To Tyson, that seemed a stretch. He had to speak up.

→ Man, Stefan, that could be asking too much! I feel like that's such a huge load to put on anybody, especially somebody as imperfect as I am.

→ No, Tyson, this is not some unbearable burden on your back. It is not some impossible rule or regulation. This is the Lord's loving invitation for you to become a true man yourself—by following the true manly example of Jesus in every way. And it is the only way you can ever be free to pray as Jesus prayed.

1:26 A.M.

Tyson had noticed that Stefan seemed to know a lot of Scriptures, so he asked him why. Stefan answered this way:

→ How else can I remember my Lord's loving words and treasure them? I have already learned by heart all of John's Gospel and many of the Psalms as well. Now I can take them with me wherever I go. I never have to lose touch with them.

→ Couldn't you just carry a Bible?

→ No, I do not own a Bible, though I hope to inherit my father's copy someday. Do you have your own Bible, Brother Tyson?

→ Yes. I have three.

→ Three! *Three Bibles!* You must be in a wealthy family indeed, or the son of the highest nobleman!

→ No, we're not nobles, and we don't own much really. But—well, anyway, I do have three Bibles.

→ What vast treasure you have! Sweet and priceless treasure! But then—Brother Tyson, I don't understand why you have asked *me* about the truths of Jesus and prayer. Don't you live every moment you can in the writings on those wonderful pages, to learn these things yourself?

→ To be honest Stefan, I suppose I haven't spent as much time in those pages as I should have.

→ Then you truly must waste no further time listening to *me*, Brother Tyson. Open your

Great Book at once! Find the words of Jesus and the works of Jesus and the ways of Jesus. Pray those things for yourself and for me and for everyone you love. Do it now, before another hour is lost.

→ But Stefan! You agreed to teach me.

A pause. It looked like Stefan was gathering his words again for a tough comeback to Tyson.

→ And yet, my brother, you seem so quick to challenge whatever I teach you, though I have tried hard to tell you only what I know is true from the Scriptures. Why spend further time disputing and question-ing these things? Why should you not rather go to the written words of the Holy Spirit, who is the one true Teacher, and who need never be questioned or chal-lenged? Why don't you seek his words instead of mine? Would this not be of infinitely more worth to you, Tyson? And would this not be a thousand times more pleasing to the Lord?

→ Hold on a minute Stefan. Have you stopped to think that maybe I don't quite understand the Scriptures as well as you do? I could use some help. I'm sorry if I question you and challenge you, but that's just how I learn the best. I know you're only fifteen (almost) just like I am, but the fact is, you sound like a college professor compared to me. Surely you've picked up on the difference between us. I must sound like a young brat to you. We're just not on the same level Stefan. So cut me some slack…I mean, be patient with me.

→ Oh, my brother, I do not mean to be impatient. My brother, will you forgive me?

→ Of course I forgive you, Stefan.

→ Brother Tyson, I have so far to go in following my Lord's example! As these hours race by for me, my mind keeps circling to Jesus in that garden, to his agony. What Jesus would be facing on the coming day was infinitely worse than anything I will ever know. And yet he was so patient with his disciples

that night. And he was gentle and silent as a
lamb the next day when he was mocked
and tortured. Why then can I not be more
patient, if these are my own final hours?
Lord Jesus, I am sorry! Forgive me for my
failure in patience! Let my last hours please
you and glorify you, my loving Lord!

It was impossible to tell it from the screen, but
Tyson sensed once more that Stefan had tears in his
eyes. He was afraid Stefan was getting too negative
and discouraged again, but he wasn't sure how to
pull him out of it.

Stefan kept going:

My brother, I am truly thankful you are here
with me. You are as much a stranger to me
as a stranger can possibly be. You call
to me from some unknown place across the
unknown sea, and from a time that has
never yet been. But you are the one the
Lord has sent to me this night, and I treasure your presence.

Tyson jumped in:

→ Stefan I should ask for your forgiveness too. I'm sorry for being so testy with you earlier, instead of listening better and learning better. Will you forgive me? And keep teaching me?

→ I forgive you, my brother. I cut you slack, as you say. And as the Lord wills, I will tell you more.

Tyson let out a breath of relief.
Stefan continued in a mood of reflection:

I was just recalling, my brother, the times I traveled to other towns with Sir Karlik.
He would often ask me to give these same seven teachings as a message to the young people we met, like a little sermon. How I loved doing that!

Stefan seemed to be reviewing his past, almost like they say you do when you're about to die—when your whole life passes in front of you. Tyson tried again to push Stefan to a brighter perspective:

→ Well Stefan, now you're preaching to me—
I'm just the latest in a long line of listeners,
with plenty more to come. So keep teaching—
it's more good practice for the future.

Stefan at last returned to the seven teachings:

→ Yes, Brother Tyson. I look again to the
stars and to the ladder. And the third
beacon and the third step that I see and
remember is simply this:

The life-story of Jesus that we are to follow
is *a life filled up with praying.*

Again and again in the wonderful pages of the
Gospels, we see Jesus praying to God the
Father. This was where Jesus received instructions for all the miracles he would do and all
the words he would teach. These things were
not his own ideas; they were what his Father
told him about while Jesus prayed.

It is so easy for me to act and speak first
and only then to pray—or to not pray at all.

But for Jesus it was always *pray* first, then act.

Think about how perfect the life of Jesus Christ appears to us—so full of great deeds and powerful words, flowing over with love and compassion and truth. Why was his life this way? Not because of some automatic perfection. But because he always looked to God in prayer to tell him what to do. More than once in John's Gospel the Savior said, "By myself, I cannot do anything." That is why Jesus kept praying. And it is why you and I must continue praying as well.

So, Brother Tyson, I keep asking the Lord to help me remember these three things:

First, Jesus was a human being just as I am.

Second, *his* life-story is *my* life-story.

And third, a Christly life is filled with prayer about everything—prayer first, action later.

Tyson congratulated himself for listening quietly to this. Actually, Stefan's words were coming together more clearly now in Tyson's mind. They were making more sense.

Stefan added this:

And do not forget, Tyson, as we continue through these seven teachings, how I link each of them to one of the seven stars in the Great Dipper. Perhaps you should do this also. Can you see this constellation from where you are?

Tyson started to explain how the light pollution from the city lights all around his house made it hard to see the stars. *No, keep it simple,* he told himself.

→ I'm actually not able to see those stars right now, Stefan. But I know what you're talking about, and I'll even draw a picture of it here to help me remember these teachings later on. I'll draw the stars—and the ladder as well.

→ Good! Then let's continue, my brother.

→ Just a quick question first, Stefan. Not a challenge or a dispute, just a question. May I?

→ Yes, my brother. Tell me your question.

→ About that third point of yours—about praying over everything, like Jesus did. Sometimes I figure I may as well not bother praying, because my mind is filled with complaints about everything. And if I prayed honestly, it would only be a lot of selfish griping. And God for sure wouldn't like that. Isn't it better just to keep quiet when I'm in that mood?

→ No, I do not believe so.

→ Why not?

→ This is the way I view it, Brother Tyson: Our point and purpose is to learn to pray as Jesus would pray. It's true that Jesus did not bring selfish complaints to God. So how can you and I get to unselfishness and peace most quickly and effectively, when our hearts are grumbling? Will it be by burying our complaints in our heart, where they fester and breed and stain our souls with bitterness? Or will it be by bringing those complaints out in the open before God, where in the Lord's light we can more easily recognize them for what they really are? Which way do you think is best?

→ No doubt about it, Stefan. The second way makes more sense.

→ I think so too, Tyson, especially since there are many examples in Scripture of men and women of God who did exactly that. Your question, my brother, was a very good one. Thank you.

→ Cool. You're welcome!

Yes, this was going better. Tyson looked up in the flame of the low-burning candle on his shelf. He didn't feel so bewildered now about the strange and disturbing things that had happened tonight. It was amazing how a little concentration on Jesus and the Bible could have such a calming effect. It gave him a lot of confidence about Stefan's situation as well, though Tyson couldn't explain why. He prayed: *Lord God, keep protecting Stefan, and get him out of that tower safely.*

Then Tyson shot this quick message to his new friend:

→ You know, Stefan, your teaching has been really good for me. I want to thank you. And I want you to know I've already been praying for you.

→ My dear Brother Tyson, nothing means more to me.

2:07 A.M.

Tyson yawned. His body felt wiped out, but his mind still seemed alert. He sent Stefan his next words:

→ Let's keep going. What's next?

But there was no answer on the screen. Why? *What was happening to Stefan?*

Tyson would just have to wait.

His candle flame started to sputter. Tyson thought about Jared's mom and her candles. Where was she at this moment? And what was Adam up to? What was going through his troubled mind? How were Natalie and Jared right now? Were they still worried and afraid?

Probably so.

Then what would Jesus pray for them?

In the room's darkness, Tyson felt around beneath his bed and found his Bible. One of his three, though he wasn't sure where the other two were. By the fading candlelight, he opened the Bible up to Matthew, to where the words in red letters started. He flipped a few pages, and spotted the place where Jesus taught his disciples to pray. He read those words from Jesus, and made them his own as he prayed out loud.

"Father in heaven, hallowed be your name, your kingdom come. Yes, Father God, let your kingdom come to us here. Be the King in Jared's life, and in Natalie's, and for Jared's mom, and even for Adam. Be the King in their lives and let them see it in a big new way tonight.

"Your kingdom come, your will be done. What is your will for them? I don't know. I know you want to love them, God. I know you want to care for them. Show your care and your love to Jared's mom, wherever she is. Show your love to Adam and Natalie and Jared. I know you want to protect them. Get them out of the devil's way, especially Adam. Get him away from those friends that bring him down.

"God, I'm sorry I didn't say all the right things to Jared and Natalie. I'm sorry I didn't follow through on praying for them like I said I would. God, I don't know what this might have cost them, but I ask you to make up for it. Make up for my mistakes, and help me make up for them too.

"And God—for Stefan, and for Juliana… O God, I don't know really what to pray, except to ask you to take care of them. What will happen to them? Show me how I can help them."

The candle's flame went out, and a last wisp of smoke drifted upward.

Next to the spent candle, Tyson saw the unfolded paper with his history assignment.

Bells. Here he'd been speaking through a thousand-year-old bell for much of the night, yet he still knew so little about them. Stefan hadn't helped much on that.

Tyson did an online search and quickly found lots of good information. Bells made from metal went back thousands of years. They have been used all over the world to sound warnings of disasters or approaching enemies, to announce great events and celebrations, and to call people to prayer.

In centuries past, they were especially used for announcing the passing of hours, back when clocks were too expensive for everyone to own one. In fact, our word *clock* came from the Latin word *cloca,* which means "bell."

Bells and time, Tyson thought—*quite a combination.* After all, Tyson was discovering that the right

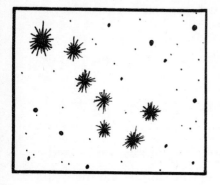

bell could even mysteriously mark off exactly a thousand years!

Tyson kept reading, and he learned all about the vibrations that give a bell its sound when you strike it. The process of creating different bells that produce different musical notes was a technology that had been extensively improved in the last thousand years. But for the bell's original purpose—to make a loud sound to get everybody's attention all around—bells still operated the same way they always had.

Yes, this could make a good report, Tyson thought. He started writing, and the words came together quickly.

Minutes later, a message finally came from Stefan with scary news:

➜ Brother Tyson, more of the Marmeccans have come here. About twenty of them, mounted like the others. How my heart trembled to see them ride into the courtyard! They have finally moved on just now, riding toward Balantiere, and leaving behind only the first four men who came earlier. So I breathe easier, though our danger continues.

Those raiders who are riding on to Balantiere are doubtless unaware that they will soon meet battle there with Sir Karlik and his men, and certain defeat. Perhaps the fight will begin even before dawn. And I will miss it. I had longed for something better.

Did you know, Brother Tyson, that my name means "crown"? But not a king's crown. "Stefan" is a champion's crown, a victor's crown, like the ivy wreath for the winner after a competition. On the day we left Bamberg and I rode south alongside Sir Karlik, I had strong hopes that I could finally begin to live up to my name in the battle about to come. But now I see that I must be a champion in some other way.

Brother Tyson, I have been praying more desperately in these last several moments. I have wanted to shout my urgent plea to God, the way Jesus so often did. Did you know that? In the Great Book, in the words to the Hebrews, it says that Jesus offered up many prayers and askings in the days of his flesh, and he did it with loud cries and tears. That is the way my heart has wanted to pray in this hour. The tears have flowed freely enough, but here I cannot shout my cry to the heavens as I wish.

And while I was praying with quiet tears, I have sensed in my heart that this is not yet the time for Juliana to leave this world. She will be safe, by the Lord's will. *Yes, O God, protect her!* But for me, I cannot find this same assurance. For me, my heart still fears that the hour to die is near.

No, Tyson thought. That couldn't be.

➔ Stefan, you can't give up hope!

→ But Brother Tyson, my best hope is
stronger than ever! So very soon, so much
sooner than I believed possible, I may be
face-to-face with my Jesus, my Savior, my
Master, my Gifter, my God! He alone is my
real hope and my highest happiness.

Tyson just couldn't believe there was no escape
from that tower for *both* Stefan and Juliana. He would
refuse to accept anything else, no matter how depress-
ing Stefan's thoughts and words became.

→ Stefan, please go ahead with those other
teachings you promised me. I've been praying—for my friends here, and for you. I know
your words are helping me!

→ Yes, my brother Tyson, I will continue.

In the stars and on the ladder, the next
teaching, the fourth teaching is this: Jesus
kept praying because this was how he
stayed in touch with his Father's *love*.
His motivation in prayer was never selfish
desire; his motivation was always love for

his Father. For Jesus, *prayer was love* and *love was prayer.*

That is why Jesus prayed with those tears and those piercing and passionate cries— because he loved his Father so intensely, so fervently. As our Master walked on earth and healed the people and taught them, he was never conscious of anything less than being totally loved by his Father. And that love kept drawing him close—to pray and pray and pray.

Never forget that, Tyson. After all, we cannot truly understand *what* Jesus would pray without also pondering *how* he would pray and *why.*

So. Brother Tyson, as you ask what Jesus would pray, make yourself strong with these teachings:

Jesus was a man as you are a man...

His life-story is your life-story...

His life was filled with prayer...

And his prayer was filled with love.

At his desk, Tyson jotted down these words on the paper where he'd drawn the Big Dipper's stars and a ladder with seven rungs.

→ I'm getting this all down, Stefan. Keep going!

Stefan did:

→ Thank you for your encouragement, my brother. And now the fifth beacon-star and the fifth step: The prayers of Jesus were filled not only with love but also with *trust.*

Jesus kept teaching his disciples that to trust is to believe, and if we believe, we will receive. He said this: "All things whatsoever that you may ask in prayer, if you ask *believing*, you will receive."

And here is the most important thing to believe God for and to trust him for:

He actually *hears* our prayer. If we don't really believe that, our true praying will only shrivel up and die. We will stop praying altogether unless we are absolutely certain that our good and loving Father is actually listening.

Stefan's words drifted into a prayer:

So Jesus my Lord, I ask you to help me pray as you would pray. Engrave my mind with these teachings, like carvings in stone. And help me not forget:

That you were a man as I am a man.

That your story is my story.

That your life was soaked in prayer.

That it was love that ignited your prayer.

And that your prayer was alive with trust.

Before going on with the seven teachings, Stefan asked Tyson out of the blue what he believed about dreams. Tyson yawned and answered, "I believe I could use some right about now. Why do you ask?"

For some reason, Stefan decided to tell Tyson about an unforgettable dream he'd had a few weeks earlier.

He had seen a great expanse of water, a warm, golden sea, and those waters were healing waters. Floating upon the sea was a cross—a huge cross made of massive timbers. It was as heavy as metal, yet it floated.

Then Stefan saw a giant hand rising up and lifting the cross out of the waters, and carrying it up and away from sight. Finally the cross came down, but it descended not in the sea, but on hard, stony ground.

"What do you think this dream means?" Stefan had asked. But Tyson couldn't guess. He was afraid to guess. He wished he could see Stefan's face so he could know at a glance how Stefan felt about the dream. Was he worried? Excited? Intrigued?

Tyson found himself suddenly longing to be with Stefan in person, to hear his actual voice, to see him face-to-face. Tyson figured that Stefan's eyes were alive with fire when he talked about Jesus and the Great Book. And Tyson wanted to hear more.

→ Stefan, we've got two more stars, two more ladder-steps to go. Tell me all about them.

Stefan put his dream aside.

→ Yes, Brother Tyson, I can still see the Great Dipper up there, though it has wheeled around in its nightly course through the sky. I think of these last two teachings as the two stars on the end of the Dipper's handle, at the place where the drinker would hold his hand. This, I believe, is where we must get the tightest grip on these truths.

And on the ladder, we are nearing the top and the highest goal of our climb.

The sixth star and the sixth step is this: All the prayers of Jesus were followed by his obedience. Whatever the Father showed him in prayer, Jesus obeyed—every instruction, every command.

To do his Father's will was his joy, and his passion, and his pursuit. Jesus said, "I seek not my will, but the will of the One who sent me." And remember what he told his Father three times in Gethsemane? "Not my will, but your will be done."

You see, Tyson, our prayer is not really complete until after the work is done—the work that God shows us to do while we pray and as we reflect on the Scriptures.

For me, this is the hardest of the stars to keep in sight, the hardest of the steps to take. But the other stars and the other steps mean nothing if we do not also embrace this one.

And now I go to the last star and the last step—we have reached it at last, my friend and brother. And here we find the simplest answer and the best answer to the question, *What would Jesus pray?*

The highest and deepest prayer that Jesus spoke to his Father was this: "Glorify your name."

You know, Brother Tyson, there was a moment, only a day before Jesus died, when he was with the people in the crowded streets of Jerusalem. He knew how very soon he would die, and his soul was troubled. "The hour has come," he said. And he looked up to heaven and spoke these words: "Father, glorify your name." That was the prayer he made in this dark and heavy moment. It was the most important prayer he could offer then, and the most important prayer you and I could ever offer as well.

Our most valuable and useful request to give to God is about *him*, not us. And that request is this: "Glorify your name."

Tyson felt he was getting a bit lost again in Stefan's deep theology. How could a guy so young be so smart?

→ Okay Stefan, I've heard that word GLORIFY a lot in worship songs and sermons. But I have to admit I don't really understand it.

→ Yes, Tyson, to understand this word is never easy for us, it seems. Glory is something we so rarely rise up to ourselves— maybe that is why we think so dimly about it.

Here is how I have learned to see it: *Glory* is what makes someone unforgettable and famous. *Glory* is the reputation that comes because of great deeds and actions. *Glory* is the song you sing and the story you tell about a hero. And *glory* is also like the light that radiates up from the eastern horizon because the sun has begun to make a new morning.

So when we ask God to glorify himself, we're asking him to do more great deeds that make him even more unforgettable and famous. We're asking him to once more show himself a hero, so we can sing about him with a new song, and tell about him with a new story. We're asking him to show us a new sunrise.

What would Jesus pray? The best answer and the purest answer that I see in the Bible is this: In every situation, the most important thing Jesus would ask his Father is this: "Glorify your name." You and I can go no higher than that.

So tell me, Tyson. Those seven stars and seven steps—how well do you remember them?

Tyson glanced at his drawing as he named them off:

→ First, Jesus was a human being just as I am.

Second, the life of Jesus is my life. His story is my story. That's why everything he prayed is what I can pray.

Third, the life Jesus lived was a life filled with prayer. He prayed about everything, just as we can. Prayer first, action later.

Number four, his prayers were always motivated by love for his Father. That should be our motive as well.

And five, his prayers were filled with trust in his Father. That can be true for us too—trusting God especially to always hear our prayer, because of his goodness and love.

Six, all his prayers were followed by full obedience to God's will. It ought to be that way for us as well.

And seven, the most important prayer Jesus made is this: "Father, glorify your name." Which means God showing himself a hero with more great deeds that make him unforgettable. For all of us, that's the simplest and best answer to the question *What would Jesus pray?*

Stefan commended Tyson. "You know them well!" he said. "Now let me help you own them. Let's use these seven things to help us pray for the friends you mentioned earlier—the ones who need desperate prayer."

At Stefan's request, Tyson told him more about his friends and the trouble they were in. He tried to explain it carefully and quickly, without bringing in modern details that would only confuse the picture for Stefan.

"There's Natalie," Tyson explained. "Her brother helped some other guys steal some things from a house. Then they burned the house down. No one else knows they did it, except Natalie. She found out and then told me. But now her brother knows that she told me, so I'm in this thing up to my ears.

"Then there's Jared. His mom is a widow, and she had only two sons. The older son just died in a horrible accident. Now both Jared and his mom are hurting really bad. And Jared's mom has gone away somewhere tonight and Jared doesn't know where. He's worried sick."

Stefan asked Tyson if any of these four people were Christians. Tyson had to say he honestly didn't know.

"Then we must pray about that as well, shouldn't we?" Stefan said. He led the way in praying for them.

He thanked Jesus for coming to earth as a man, and for facing all the same temptations that Adam and Natalie and Jared and Jared's mom were facing.

Stefan thanked Jesus for showing us how to live and how to pray, and he asked God to open the eyes of Tyson's friends to see this.

He thanked Jesus for living a life filled with prayer, and he asked that Adam and Natalie and Jared and Jared's mom would begin filling up their lives that way too, by turning to Jesus and asking God for salvation from their sin.

Stefan went on: "Thank you, Jesus, for your love for your Father, and for giving me a taste of that same love. I love you, Lord, and that is why I ask for you to do wonderful deeds in these four lives.

"I fully trust that you hear my prayer and will answer.

"Show me what to do, and show Tyson what to do, so that we can help Adam and Natalie and Jared and Jared's mother. And we will obey whatever you show us.

"I ask you again: Prove yourself a hero in their lives. Do something tonight for Adam, for Natalie, for Jared, and for Jared's mother that will show them who you really are. Do something for them tonight that they can never forget."

After they prayed, Stefan told Tyson that he was looking into the night sky and that the stars were becoming hidden.

"Clouds are moving in," he said. "I may never see sunshine on this earth again."

Then these words came:

→ Brother Tyson, I am leaving Juliana alone here for just a moment. I haven't awakened her to explain this to her, but I want you to know.

→ What are you doing, Stefan? Where are you going?

→ Don't worry, Tyson. I must take something down below, and also bring something else back here. I must go slowly and quietly. But I promise I will return.

A spark of hope was kindled in Tyson's mind.

→ Stefan, wait! Before you go, tell me: You've got an idea, don't you? A plan for getting out of there alive?

But Stefan was already gone.

3:19 A.M.

After Stefan went away, Tyson battled his weariness and continued to get more work done on his history report. It was shaping up well; he thought he would finish it soon.

Then a message came from Jared.

> → hey tyson glad to see you still there i have great news for you. my mom is back and i thank god for that. thank you for your prayers, i just know you were praying.
>
> you won't believe what happened. i dont know why i didnt think of this before but the place she went to was the cemitery. she went to scotts grave. thats where she took the candles. she went out there and lit the candles and she told me she prayed and gave scott into the hands of god, and she also thanked god that she still has me. she cried a

lot out there and she is still crying some since she got home but its like a different kind of crying now. i cried some with her, actually a lot when she first walked in the door, i was so glad to see her. :)

but heres what you really wont believe. while mom was out there someone walked up to her and really scared her at first. youll never guess who it was. it was adam kohek. he had been out wandering around pretty mixed up about something i guess, from what mom said. he had parked his car at the cemitery gate and was out walking alone when he saw moms candle, so he went over to talk. he told my mom that he was in some heavy trouble, so mom talked about losing her own son and how short life is and not to waste it or do anything you regret later. i dont know what kind of problem adam has but maybe my mom helped him out. and mom said she felt so much better after talking with him.

this has been a long nite tyson but good after all. i am crashing now will try to get a

little sleep anyway. see you in history class
and i hope you finished your paper

and thanks for all you do for me. :)

Unbelievable, Tyson thought. No—it *was* believable, thanks to God.

A message from Natalie was right behind Jared's:

→ Tyson, I've got to let you know. Adam
never came home, but I got a phone call a
short while ago. He turned himself in to the
police, and he's there now at the station.
After I found out, I phoned my dad, and he's
on his way home right away.

We don't know what will happen next for
Adam. Whatever it is, I'm sure it won't be
easy. But maybe this is the start of something
better than I ever thought was possible.

I feel I owe you a big thank you—you must
have been praying because I feel like a miracle
happened somehow in Adam's mind last night
after he left home, though I don't know how.

I probably won't make it to school tomorrow. I mean today, that is. I want to sleep some and wait here for Dad. But I'll talk with you soon. :-]

When Tyson finished reading their messages, he jumped from his chair and let out a whoop of praise to God—though it turned partly into a shout of pain when he again felt his side injury. Maybe Stefan wasn't able to get loud with the Lord right now, but Tyson sure could.

He looked forward to talking with both Jared and Natalie and letting them know what he was learning about God. He had no idea how he could ever explain about Stefan and the bell. No one would believe him. He would just have to leave that part out. But that was okay. Besides, he knew Stefan wouldn't mind remaining unknown. Stefan would want to make sure God was the hero of this story.

And Stefan would want Tyson to use all that had happened as an opportunity to talk with his friends about the biggest heroic deed ever—how Jesus had died for their sins and defeated death. Tyson didn't know exactly how to talk with them about this, but he knew he had to try, and he shot up a prayer to ask for God's help.

With the end of this long night not far away, all Tyson needed now to give him absolutely total joy was to find out more from Stefan about his plan... and then see it through to success.

4:01 A.M.

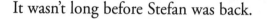

It wasn't long before Stefan was back.

→ I've returned, Brother Tyson, as I promised.

→ Stefan, what were you doing? What's your plan?

→ Brother Tyson, I believe I know why I had that dream I told you about. Last evening, when I selected books to read, I glanced at the iron cross on the schoolroom wall down below. I know the raiders have noticed it too. It is as big as my hand, and quite thick and heavy. That is what I went down below to get. And I left my dagger and staff down there. I will explain why.

This is my plan: When the light of dawn comes, and when I am sure that the raiders are not looking this way, I will toss that cross up into the air and let it fall onto the cobbles beside their fire. These pagans are full of superstition, and they might even suspect that this cross has fallen upon them from the stormy sky. They will be afraid to pick it up. They will circle around it in shock, unsure of what to do.

Meanwhile I will have quickly slipped down the tower stairs and taken up the weapons that are waiting for me beside the door. I will step boldly into the open courtyard. In the name of my God I will challenge these offenders, then rush upon them with the dagger in my right hand and the staff in my left.

That is my plan.

Tyson gulped. Then he wrote:

→ You said CHALLENGE them? You mean you'll actually talk to them? But Stefan, that will take away the surprise. Can't you at least try to sneak up on them?

→ No, Tyson. To do that is the pagan way. The way of a knight is the way of honor, and honor demands that a knight must first present the challenge. Yet even then, with one against four, I believe I stand a good chance of killing or maiming them all, no matter what it costs me. For I will fight to the death if I must. And I am determined that Juliana will be safe.

This idea did not sound like a guaranteed winner. But Tyson sensed that he need not argue with Stefan about it. His friend's mind was set. Besides, what other options were there?

The more he thought about it, the more Tyson worried.

→ Stefan, after you go down there and challenge those guys, what if you don't—I mean what if the raiders—I mean what if you're injured? And you won't be able to get back up the tower stairs to talk with me? How will I find out what happened? How will I know how you are?

Stefan didn't answer the question. He spoke these words instead:

→ Now all I do is wait for light. Tyson—I want you to pray for me. Will you do that? I want to pray silently now, alone. I have so much to plead with God about. My heart is overwhelmed with the desire to feel the warmth of the sunshine on my face again, and yet I do not know that I ever will. I will step away from the bell now and lie on my face on the landing floor, and pray. And as I do, I would like to know that you are still there, Tyson, so close to me, even from a thousand years away. I would like to know that you are interceding for me. Tyson, this would mean more to me than I can express. Will you stay awake and do this for me?

→ Yes Stefan—I will pray.

Tyson leaned back slowly in his chair. Then he slipped out of it and dropped to his knees on the floor beside his bed. He couldn't keep tears from forming in his eyes. He felt as if Stefan had become his closest friend on earth tonight. He almost laughed aloud through his tears to think about that one—his closest friend right now was a millennium away!

Tyson prayed. If ever there was a time for God to prove himself a hero in Stefan's life, this seemed like it. He asked God to glorify himself. That was still a huge, mysterious concept to Tyson in lots of ways, but also a very exciting one.

Tyson thought about love for God being the fuel for his prayer. He thought about trusting him enough to really believe God was hearing his prayer. He thought about these things, and as he did, he talked about them with God.

But then he stopped praying. He started imagining the worst. Stefan would follow his plan, but Tyson was afraid not everything would go exactly as he wanted—not quite.

Tyson's imagination threw him back again into the olden days of knights. It all seemed more real than ever in Tyson's mind. He saw himself riding away from a battle in the north, with his wounded side aching. He rode into the city of Bamberg, straight to the palace of King Henry. He dismounted, and hurried in. The king's great hall was filled with people, but they were all silent and no one was smiling. Tyson stood between Sir Karlik and Brother Brendan as the king rose from his throne and read from a piece of parchment:

> *Be it hereby established*
> *in this realm that great*
> *reverence and lasting honor be*
> *accorded to the name and memory of*
> *Stefan son of Dedrick of Blue*
> *Mountain in Loudriana.*

> *For as a squire in humble service to*
> *his lord Sir Karlik of Bamberg,*
> *and in faithfulness to his appointed*
> *duty, Squire Stefan saved the life of the*
> *child Juliana, daughter of Brendan*
> *of Gronza, even unto the*
> *slaying of four barbarians who would*
> *otherwise have burned*
> *alive both Stefan and Juliana.*

In this heroic deed, by battling
the barbarians to save the child, Squire
Stefan received mortal wounds.
He is with us no more.
His soul has been commended
to God, whom he dearly loved,
and his body has been laid to rest in
the courtyard below the bell tower
of the fortress of Gronza, the very same
courtyard where Stefan received
the blows that took his life.

Therefore be it ordered
by royal decree that the bell in the
tower of Gronza be sounded every
morning at dawn in the memory of
Squire Stefan, for as long as
the glory of the sun shall shine by day
and the silent stars by night.

No, Tyson told himself, *you're letting your imagi-*
nation run away with you. Tyson forced himself to

shut off this kind of thinking. *Besides,* he told himself, *it's not about Stefan's glory anyway. God is the hero!* Tyson dropped his head onto the bed and started praying again for Stefan's protection...until his thoughts drifted away into drowsiness and sleep.

5:19 A.M.

Tyson awoke with a start. He popped up his head from the bed, and checked the display on his clock. 5:19.

He hurried to the chair at his desk, and jiggled his mouse to get the snow-boarder action-shot screen saver to disappear.

→ Stefan. Stefan! STEFAN!

There was no answer.

Tyson tried to bury the thought that he might never hear from Stefan again.

He heard his parents in the kitchen, ready to leave for work. Tyson went in to tell them good morning. He thanked his dad for his prayers about the report—and for the good idea behind it.

Tyson's mom looked more energetic than he'd seen her in a while, and her eyes were alive with brightness. Tyson moved close to give her a hug before she stepped out the door. Then he experienced something he had never known while hugging her before: He found himself silently praying for her, asking God to help her feel strong today, without her back hurting.

After his parents left, Tyson hurried back to his room. He looked out his bedroom window and saw the dawn's faint light. It was going to be a cloudy, murky morning. Looking to the sky, he prayed again for Stefan. Would he never hear from his friend again?

He glanced over again to his computer screen, and saw this:

→ I am here, Brother Tyson.

Tyson rushed to his keyboard.

→ Stefan, what's happening?

→ Juliana still sleeps. The sky's light is growing behind thick clouds, which look very stormy. I feel as if the morning is taking a deep breath before unleashing a terrible blast of wind and rain. The first morning birds are singing, and some are flying, but they swoop low, as if expecting raindrops or hailstones to fall any moment.

Stefan sounded calm, and Tyson was grateful for that. But was he still in danger?

→ And down in the courtyard, Stefan. The raiders. What do you see?

→ All four are stoking the fire, and they make torches for setting the buildings ablaze. They do not like the look of this murky sky. It makes them uneasy. I sense that they are well ready to leave this place. I think they will not bother with any plundering. They will just set their fires and go. Already their torches are being lit.

→ Stefan—time's getting short!

→ Yes, my brother. The light has grown. I must not wait any longer. The time has come.

→ Stefan! BROTHER Stefan—God be with you, my friend. God be your hero!

→ And also yours, my brother. Farewell.

Tyson stayed by his computer screen, staring. Outside, rain began falling, and soon it was a heavy downpour, thrashing Tyson's window. Thunder rumbled in the distance.

The minutes hurried by, way too fast. Each time Tyson looked at his clock, his spirits sank a little more. But still he stayed at his desk, waiting and hoping. 5:33. 5:49. 6:03. 6:22. 6:47. 7:07. Soon Tyson would have to leave for school.

The rain kept pouring, but Tyson could envision the sun's rays lighting up the tops of the storm clouds.

He stepped away from his desk and fell on his bed again, facing upward. He looked again at his Slickrock Trail poster.

For the first time, Tyson counted the bikers trekking in single file across the huge bare rocks in the picture's foreground. Seven. He also counted the number of the rocky red peaks standing out in the far background. Seven.

That's good, he thought, staring into the picture. *This will be a perfect reminder to pray Stefan's way. That is—Jesus' way.* Tyson mentally tagged each of the peaks and each of the bikers in the picture with one of Stefan's teachings.

But he was afraid those seven teachings were all that he'd ever have to remember Stefan by. Dejectedly, he looked over at his computer screen once more.

→ Brother?

Tyson had been waiting so long, it took a moment for the fact to register: A message!

He rushed to the keyboard and shot back:

→ Stefan? Is that you?

→ It's me, brother.

Tyson's heart was pounding in joy.

→ Stefan, what happened?

→ I must depart quickly, Tyson. But all is well here. I tossed the iron cross into the courtyard and heard one of the raiders scream in terror when it landed. Then just as I charged into the courtyard and ordered those Marmeccans to drop their weapons, there was a crack of lightning on the hillside above us. One of the pagans stumbled backward into the fire. Then they all did exactly what I commanded—they dropped everything and ran out the gate and down the Balantiere road.

They didn't get far before they were captured by Brother Brendan and some soldiers, who just then were returning here with a healer for Juliana.

My comrades also brought a word of blessing for me from Sir Karlik. He has ordered me to return at once to my master's side. They have cornered the other Marmeccans in the marshes by the river, and the battle will not begin until I and most of the other soldiers here have rejoined our commander.

Brother Brendan will stay for now with Juliana. We've lowered her mat down below, and the healer is already at work to set her bones.

And I must ride away this very moment, on this dark and rainy morning, though in my heart the sun blazes more brightly than ever. But before I depart, I've been ordered up to this tower one last time to ring the bell—as a warning to any raiders who might still be lurking in the woods around us. They must hear that this fortress is no longer abandoned.

So I will ring the bell. And after that I must bid you farewell, Tyson, and ride forth.

Tyson swallowed hard.

→ WAIT Stefan—maybe you shouldn't ring that bell.

→ But I am commanded to, my brother. Why should I not ring it?

→ I was just afraid that maybe if the bell is rung, my link with you could be gone. Maybe even forever.

→ Don't you have the power to restore the connection?

→ ME? Of course not Stefan. Why should I have that power?

→ I must tell you this, Brother Tyson—I keep suspecting that you really are an angel sent to test me, despite what you say.

→ Get real, Stefan! I don't come across as being that good do I?

→ No, no you do not—but it still seems easier to believe you're an angel than to believe this bell can carry human voices across a thousand years! But if you truly are *not* an angel...then as your faithful brother, I charge you, Tyson, to never forget those seven teachings. I plead with you to make the same vow to your Lord that I have made—to live the rest of your life in pursuit of this goal: to pray as Jesus prayed. Brother Tyson, I leave that charge *in your hands* to do what you know is right before God.

Tyson wanted more than ever to look into his friend's face and speak with him man to man. But all he could do was type letters on a keyboard:

→ Thank you, Brother Stefan. And what about *your* hands? Are they on that pull-rope?

→ Yes they are.

→ You're going to pull it?

→ Yes I am.

→ Before you do, Stefan— I just want to say—the Lord bless you, my brother. And may God be your hero all your days. Okay—you can pull it now.

After Tyson typed those last letters, he heard at once a thunder boom outdoors that rumbled on for ten seconds at least.

And there was nothing more from Stefan on the screen.

But Tyson didn't feel dejected anymore, even as he stood and looked out the window at the gloomy rain. He thanked God for his new friend and brother, and for the lessons Stefan had taught so well. Tyson was sure these teachings would stay in his mind and heart forever, fresh and alive.

And clear as a bell.

Seven Steps, Seven Stars

1. HUMANITY—Jesus was a human being just as I am. He prayed as a human being, just as we do.

2. LIFE-STORY—The life of Jesus is my life. His story is my story. Therefore everything he prayed is what I can pray, and should pray.

3. PRAYER-FULLNESS—Jesus lived a life filled with prayer. He prayed about everything, just as we can. Prayer first, action later.

4. LOVE—The prayers of Jesus were always motivated by love for God

his Father. This can be our motivation as well.

5. TRUST—The prayers of Jesus were filled with trust in his Father. This can and should be true for us too. We can trust God especially to *hear* our prayer out of his goodness and love.

6. OBEDIENCE—As Jesus prayed, God showed him what he wanted his Son to do. Then Jesus fully obeyed what he had learned in prayer from his Father. This is how it can also be for us.

7. GLORY FOR GOD—The most important prayer Jesus made is this: "Father, glorify your name." When God glorifies his name, he shows himself a hero with great deeds that make him unforgettable.

For all of us, that's the simplest and best answer to the question, *What would Jesus pray?*

What Would Jesus Pray? Where to Find It in the Bible

If you own a Bible, open it and look up the passages listed here. You'll get several glimpses of the prayer life of Jesus. See *what* Jesus prayed…and *when*…and *where*…and *how*….

Reflect on all these things as you read about him. Let him show you how to follow his pathway in prayer.

His Prayer Habits

Alone in a quiet place—Matthew 14:23

Early, and alone, and quiet—Mark 1:35

On a mountain—Mark 6:46

Quiet and alone—Luke 5:16

All night—Luke 6:12

Alone—Luke 9:18

By himself—John 6:15

With passion—Hebrews 5:7

Particular Prayer Times and Requests

A long time of fasting—Matthew 4:1–2

Thanksgiving for what God reveals—Matthew 11:25

Praying for children—Matthew 19:13

On the night before he died—Matthew 26:38–44
    (see also Mark 14:32–39 and Luke 22:39–46)

When he was baptized—Luke 3:21

Before choosing his 12 disciples, including Judas—
    Luke 6:12–16

Blessing food—Luke 9:16

Before a crucial teaching time—Luke 9:18–27

Before an amazing transformation—Luke 9:28–29

Before teaching about prayer—Luke 11:1

For protecting a man from Satan—Luke 22:31–32

At a dead man's grave—John 11:41–42

When he was troubled—John 12:27–28

For the Holy Spirit's coming—John 14:16–17

On the night before he died—John 17:1–26

WHAT JESUS LEARNED IN PRAYER FROM HIS FATHER

Things to do—John 5:20 and 10:32

Words to say—John 12:49, 14:10, and 17:8

Things to teach—John 8:38, 14:24, and 15:15

God's will—John 5:30

God's presence—John 8:29

His Cries from the Cross

Matthew 27:46 (also Mark 15:34)

Luke 23:34

Luke 23:46

Some of the Things Jesus Taught Us about Prayer

For God's reward—Matthew 6:5–8

A model prayer—Matthew 6:9–13 (also Luke 11:1–4)

Persistence—Luke 11:5–13 (also Matthew 7:7–11)

Pray for harvest workers—Matthew 9:35–38

About temptation—Matthew 26:41
     (also Mark 14:38)

Prayer and faith—Mark 11:22–24

Prayer and forgiving others—Mark 11:25
     (also Matthew 6:12–15)

Don't get discouraged—Luke 18:1–7

Doing great things for God—John 14:12–14

Glory for God, and fruitfulness—John 15:7–8

Getting filled with joy—John 16:24

Where to Find the Scriptures that Stefan Talked About

At 10:59 p.m.

"With the Lord, a day is as a thousand years, and a thousand years is as a day"—2 Peter 3:8

"Nothing is too difficult for the Lord"—Jeremiah 32:17 and 32:27; Mark 10:27 and 14:36; Luke 18:27

"The wonderful psalm that Solomon wrote…about the noble and righteous man"—Psalm 72

"May prayer be made for him always…" —Psalm 72:15

At 12:54 a.m.

"Train us to pray"—Luke 11:1

At 1:10 a.m.

"God is love"—1 John 4:8, 4:16

"Anyone who is claiming to live in Jesus must walk as
Jesus walked"—1 John 2:6

"He died once for all as our ransom"—1 Peter 3:18,
Matthew 20:28, Mark 10:45, Hebrews 9:15

"Because he died, we have life"—Romans 6:10–11

"Doesn't Jesus tells us to take up our cross and follow him?"—Matthew 10:38 and 16:24;
Mark 8:34; Luke 9:23 and 14:27

"With Christ I have been crucified"—Galatians 2:20

"We are *joined* with Jesus in the likeness of both his
death and his resurrection"—Romans 6:5

At 1:26 a.m.

"By myself, I cannot do anything"—John 5:19,
5:30, 8:28

At 2:07 a.m.

"Jesus offered up many prayers and askings in the
days of his flesh…with loud cries and tears"
—Hebrews 5:7

"If we believe, we will receive"—Matthew 21:22,
Mark 11:24

At 2:50 a.m.

"I seek not my will, but the will of the One who
sent me"—John 5:30, 6:38

"The hour has come"—John 12:27

"Father, glorify your name"—John 12:28